CHRISTMAS IN THE HIGHLANDS

Anthology With 2 Stories

MADELYN HILL

D0556283

SOUL MATE PUBLISHING

New York

CHRISTMAS IN THE HIGHLANDS

Copyright©2016

MADELYN HILL

Cover Design by Anna Lena-Spies

Published in the United States of America by
Soul Mate Publishing
P.O. Box 24
Macedon, New York, 14502

ISBN: 978-1-68291-484-7

ebook ISBN: 978-1-68291-291-1

www.SoulMatePublishing.com

What Readers are saying about Madelyn Hill's novels ~

"What a promising debut novel (Wolf's Castle) for a talented new author! There is obviously a rich store of possibilities in storytelling ahead." *InD'tale Magazine*

"WOLF'S CASTLE is a quick romantic read with a little bit of everything: betrayal, heartbreak, secrets, lies, romance and a little sex. If you are a fan of the historical Scottish romance where the leading man is reluctant to fall in love and struggles with His own demons, then Wolf's Castle is ideal read for a lazy afternoon." *The Reading Café*

"HEATHER IN THE MIST is full of betrayal, adventure and romance in a Scottish highland setting this story is electric! Rogan is a strong-willed lass who keeps her faith in love while Ian is honorable and courageous, *tempting both the reader and Rogan at every turn*. A number of surprising twists with perilous adventure will have one's adrenaline pumping while the moments of romance filled with passion and emotion will have one's heart-a-flutter." *InD'tale Magazine* March 2016 **Nominated for the coveted InD'Tale's 2016 RONE Award!**

Books by Madelyn Hill

Wolf's Castle
For the Love of a Gypsy
Heather in the Mist
Highland Hope
Christmas in the Highlands

I'd like to dedicate this anthology

to my editor Char Chaffin.

When I submitted the stories

for a completely different project,

she saw promise and encouraged me to flesh out

the one short story into two novellas.

Her guidance and her editing expertise

have helped me to continue to perfect my writing craft.

Acknowledgements

Anyone who knows me or visits during the Holiday Season, knows that Christmas is my favorite holiday. I love the decorating, baking, and togetherness. So, now with two decorated trees, an endless Christmas village, and trays and trays of cookies, the season continues to be a magical time of year.

When Soul Mate Publishing was looking to create a Christmas Anthology, I was very excited. Although, my story isn't in the anthology, I was encouraged to extend my first short story into two novellas and thus, Christmas in the Highlands was born.

BOOK ONE

A FAMILY FOR CHRISTMAS

Chapter 1

Scottish Highlands – Gordon Territory
1710

Bollocks.

Malcolm Sutherland inhaled sharply.

His betrothed took his breath away.

Lady Rossalyn Gordon was like the faeries rumored to inhabit the Highlands during the time of gnomes and trolls. Her eyes twinkled with a magical gleam, much like the crystal blue of the firth as the sun hit the cresting waves.

Aye, sparkling gems of blue.

Her wedding gown swept over her curves, caressing her lush breasts, tiny waist, and the slope of full hips. A swath of the clan plaid draped over one shoulder, a true Highland lass. He smiled, more than pleased with her appearance.

"Laird Malcolm Sutherland, I give ye me daughter, Lady Rossalyn Gordon," Laird Gordon boomed.

The man seemed extraordinarily pleased with himself. Malcolm's instincts flared. Did they hum because of the beautiful Lady Rossalyn? Or because he didn't trust her father?

Laird Gordon slapped him on the back. His dark eyes scrutinized Malcolm's every move as if he were waiting for him to flee or else beat the shite out of him.

Malcolm held his ground and stared at the man without letting any emotion show. He needed to be strong. He needed the alliance and damned if Gordon didn't ken this fact. And use the fact his clan needed food stores as a way to bargain.

Aye, the betrothal was quick, unexpected by the poor lass, but she'd relented. And, according to Gordon, seemed pleased to be marrying into the Sutherland clan. Malcolm hadn't been privy to the conversation between Gordon and his daughter. But in the end all that mattered was their nuptials.

His people depended on the alliance and as laird, Malcolm's duty was to protect and provide.

The lady backed away now, her eyes wary. The black curls of her coiffure slipped out of their knot, tangling around her face fetchingly. A swift shot of lust arrowed straight to his cods. *Damn*, he didn't want to feel desire for her—she was a means to an end, a way to secure the future of his clan—no matter how bewitching she was.

Within a thrice, Laird Gordon was at her side. Pain wreathed her face as her father gripped her arm. Gordon looked over his shoulder with an angry scowl, and Malcolm moved forward as he reached for his broadsword. His men came to attention, metal scraping against metal as they drew their weapons.

What kind of man inflicted pain on his own daughter?

The laird held up his hand and grinned. "No need, Sutherland. The lass is shy, 'tis all." He winked. "Maiden sensibilities, to be sure."

She cast Gordon a loathing look. It appeared as if his daughter held him in low esteem. Mayhap Malcolm should have waited for another option, a different alliance for his clan. But he'd tried and Gordon was the only laird willing to agree to the contract.

After a moment, Malcolm slipped the sword back into the scabbard secured along his back, nodding to his men. They stayed their actions, but still stood at attention.

He looked to Lady Rossalyn. Color had returned to her face, shading her cheeks with a rosy hue. Aye, she was lovely—fresh, innocent. 'Twas what he'd demanded. Gordon and the keep's doctor had sworn an oath promising her chastity.

He'd not be fooled again.

She pushed past her father and stood before Malcolm, her gaze sweeping over him. He smirked, and her eyes snapped to his face, anger darkening those orbs to midnight blue. Her ire encouraged him. While he didn't wish to wed a shrew, he was more than happy with a strong woman at his side.

Gordon approached and wrapped his arm around her shoulders. "Lass, 'tis time to be wed."

Her jaw clenched and Malcolm swore she was ready to yell at the man, but her father merely held her gaze, until apparently he'd won the battle of wills. Lady Rossalyn sighed as she glanced up at Gordon, and uncertainty filled her gaze.

Malcolm nearly moved forward to sweep her into his arms. He didn't give in to the impulse—he wasn't a romantic man, subject to ideas of whimsy—but for some reason, once he spied Lady Rossalyn he'd been thinking decidedly romantic thoughts.

"Aye, Father, I'm ready."

Ah, her voice, soft, slightly husky. Sensual.

Damn, he was ready to consummate the marriage before they were legally wed.

She trembled a bit as their eyes met. She lowered her gaze until her lashes cast a shadow against the pale skin of her cheeks. When she lifted her eyes again, resolve and a bit of stubbornness filled them. Malcolm nearly laughed, but checked his impulse.

Now wasn't the time for laughter.

In a few moments, they'd both pledge to honor and obey. And then, their fates would be sealed.

Marriage? To a stranger? Rossalyn's mind raced to find a solution before she spoke her vows.

None came. Quite the contrary, all reasoning supported the union. She only sought a safe place to live, away from the hovel in which she'd faced many indignities. And now one last indignity was thrust upon her by her father—an unexpected marriage. Which was particularly hard at the current time of year and all the memories it wrought.

'Twas the time of celebration with Christmas fast approaching, and the anniversary of her mother's death as well. To honor her, Rossalyn longed to share her mother's love of holiday traditions and festivities in a keep which would appreciate such frivolity. Her father had loathed Christmas and all of its trappings. So much so, he forbade any acknowledgement of the season. And it broke her heart.

No matter, for as she stood next to this man—a lifeline for her—calmness settled in, easing the shaking of her hands. A quick prayer slipped through her mind . . .

Please understand. Please forgive.

The priest started the ceremony, and all too soon, had bade the laird to kiss the bride.

Dear God Almighty, he was going to kiss her. A plethora of thoughts raced through her mind. She hadn't been kissed since Daniel had been alive. Tears clogged the back of her throat. 'Twas her fault he was gone; her fault she was in this precarious position and needed saving—apparently by Laird Malcolm Sutherland.

When she'd entered the main hall, she'd nearly run back to her chamber and barred the door. But there was something about him, especially when he'd been ready to challenge her father. His swagger was determined, and she'd been completely taken with the strength of him as he'd pulled the large sword from its sheath.

Now there was a wild look to the man as his face approached hers, ready to claim her as his wife. She marveled at the hard planes of his cheeks, the strong jaw and brow. His hair flowed to his shoulders, a thick mass of dark brown, tempting her fingers to grab on and not let go.

She pulled back, searched his gaze. Aye, she recognized the look of desire and it rattled her to the core.

No matter what she thought or felt, this man was her salvation.

He slowly curled his hand behind her head, cradling her, bringing a sense of security.

A slight grin tipped up his broad mouth as she met him halfway. His lips were warm and firm as they played over hers. He pulled her flush against his strong body, slightly lifting her up onto her toes. She melted a little against the hard wall of his chest. Though a stranger, her heart found a bit of reassurance at their attraction to each other. When his hands moved on her back, then traveled down her hips, she pulled away. 'Twas too soon, too intimate.

Laird Sutherland—now her husband—brushed the back of his hand along her cheek. "Lovely," he said in a low voice, for her ears only.

Her heart pattered and she swallowed. The compliment embarrassed her as much as it pleased her. It had been so long since she'd appreciated the attention of a man. Any woman would be thrilled by his words, more so by his strength and handsome face. And how heat coursed through her body after his kiss.

She shuddered as her father abruptly pulled her to him and gave a rough hug. His foul body odor made her gag and she tried to ease from his embrace. Ah, to be away from this man—this wretched, wretched man. 'Twas as if her prayers were answered with the arrival of Laird Sutherland.

"I present Laird and Lady Sutherland," the priest intoned.

Laird Sutherland's men cheered, her father's clan also willingly rousing a few hoots of approval. Their lack of enthusiasm wasn't all that unexpected. Busy eating and indulging in ale, why would they care if she were wed?

And all she could think of was leaving her childhood home—leaving hell and her wretched memories, for mayhap a better place.

Her father had a reason to betroth her to Laird Sutherland. A good reason. Regardless, Laird Gordon was an evil man.

And the man who'd murdered Daniel . . . her first husband.

Chapter 2

Malcolm was more than ready to quit the keep and seek his home in Sutherland territory. He longed for the comfort of a clean and orderly household—with his new wife at his side.

He found the stench of the main hall, coupled with Gordon's slovenly men, putrid. Malcolm held no appetite for the light repast before leaving. 'Twasn't what he expected from a clan whose fertile soil and food bounty mocked Sutherland's stores. With all of their resources, one would think Laird Gordon possessed a thriving, industrious clan who cared for people and territory.

Should he be concerned? Despite all instinct to leave and forget the alliance, Malcolm remained for the sake of his clan. A quick glance around the main hall, and his worries flared once again. Would his new wife have the skills to care for his people? The clan depended on him to make the right choices. He needed a woman who'd be loyal, honest, and dote upon his family as if they were her own.

More importantly, Clan Sutherland needed the alliance, filled with the exchange of crops for his warriors and the promise to patrol the shared lands to ensure a rival clan didn't attempt to usurp their power. Tempers flared quickly in the Highlands. One never kenned when a clan would imagine a slight from another, and fighting would break out. Gordon needed the help of Sutherland clansmen. And Malcolm had required a wife.

Was Lady Rossalyn that woman?

God, he prayed so.

He kept an eye on her as his men lifted their cups in a toast. She seemed startled by their marriage and her brow creased with what appeared as worry. He'd relieve her of her qualms when they had a moment of privacy. He hoped 'twould be sooner than later.

Did his new wife fear him? A loathsome thought. He was a fair man and determined not to judge her because her sire seemed to be a bastard and didn't instill pride in his people.

After nodding and offering her a smile, Malcolm left the main hall and followed Gordon to his study. The room resembled the keep, filthy beyond measure. How did these people live among such squalor?

"Me daughter will do well by ye."

"Aye," Malcolm replied. She had better, or else he'd lose more than his pride, he'd also lose the trust of his men and their families. He'd pledged to find a solution to the clan's problems and when Gordon approached him, it seemed the best option for the both of them.

"I've the papers for ye to sign." Gordon poured a tumbler of whiskey and nodded to Malcolm to do the same.

Their stewards had settled the contract before Malcolm had arrived, but there were some final details he wished to confirm and approve himself.

After a quick toast, Malcolm found a chair and started sifting through the papers.

Gordon smirked.

With one hard glance, Malcolm stifled the man's rudeness. He couldn't wait to quit the keep.

"Och, 'tis no need to read them. All agreed upon items are listed," the laird said as he poured more to drink.

Did he truly think Malcolm would sign the contract without reading it through once again? His instincts hummed anew. What was the man hiding? Did he mean to trick him? His clan?

"I will read it."

Gordon's men chuckled. Ignoring them, Malcolm continued through the contract detailing their alliance. 'Twas a vile situation he'd found himself in after his parents' death. They'd readily traded with other clans, but no formal agreement was documented. After his father's passing, Malcolm had found the alliances would no longer hold and his clan would not receive the needed food stores.

When Gordon contacted him, Malcolm kenned 'twas the only option in which both clans would benefit.

After he'd read through each and every paper, he pushed them aside.

Gordon thunked his tumbler onto his desk. Ale splashed over the rim and nearly soiled the contract. "Sign them, Sutherland."

Malcolm leaned back and held up his hands. "We are not done with all of the details. First, we need to schedule the patrols and delivery of goods."

Gordon nodded and sat. "Och, we've time for that later. Sign the contract."

Why was the man so concerned? Malcom's brow arched. He'd already wed Lady Rossalyn. "We'll create a schedule or I won't sign the contract."

The laird frowned. "Aye, aye. We'll do as you say."

"My men will patrol the borders along with your men."

Gordon shifted in his seat and seemed to contemplate what Malcolm had stated. He rubbed his stubbled jaw. "I've not enough men to spare the entire winter."

"'Twas our agreement, Gordon." He glanced at the contract, resting like a poisonous snake between them. He'd not relent. Gordon needed protection and the Sutherlands needed food stores. While he loved his keep, the unforgiving terrain made for poor crops. The past few years had been particularly horrid with failed attempts at growing enough food for a clan the size of the Sutherlands.

"Och, I'll spare ten and then come spring you'll send some young lads to help with sowing the harvest."

"Aye." He'd plenty of young lads who'd do well to learn how to tend the land. Malcolm reached for the contract, wrote what they'd agreed upon, then signed and stamped his seal in hot wax.

While every instinct told him not to trust this man, each clan sought the security and resources the marriage would provide.

Wed to a woman he didn't ken. A lovely woman, truth be told—a beauty. Yet, she could be a shrew for all his knowledge of her. Was he bargaining his future happiness in order to provide for his family? Not that he'd revealed to his people the uncertainty in which he'd made this agreement. They'd only see a happily married laird and lady and if Gordon held his word, enough food so they wouldn't go hungry.

"Grand. 'Twill be good for both clans," Gordon said as he rose. A smile creased his aged face. "Celebrate, while I say goodbye to me dear daughter." As Gordon left the chamber, he turned and waved a slight salute in Malcolm's direction. With a flash of a wink, the man was gone.

Some of his men followed. Others remained and poured more whiskey or ale. They lounged and kicked up their feet upon the desk and other furniture.

Malcolm momentarily thought to follow Gordon as his behavior before the ceremony came to him. How he'd grabbed his daughter and acted in anger. He rose and went to the hallway outside the office. "Gordon," he called to the man.

The laird stopped at the end of the hall and turned to face Malcolm.

"Would you like me to accompany you?" He was trying to be polite but firm as well.

Gordon waved at him. "Och, 'tis me daughter and I'd

like a few minutes alone with her to wish her good luck with her new husband and clan."

While he doubted the man often wished his daughter well, there was naught Malcolm could do but nod and say, "Aye."

He reentered the study. As he observed Gordon's men, more doubt filled his mind. He needed crops. These men looked as if they hadn't worked in ages. If Gordon was going to live up to his promise and the signed documents upon his desk, who did he have working for him? Obviously, not these men or any Malcolm had encountered during his brief stay.

Och, but instinct plagued him, yet he needed to ready his own men and ensure they were equipped to handle the long journey ahead.

He studied the papers, doubting their veracity. But he'd read every word and 'twas what was agreed, promised. Rubbing the back of his neck, Malcolm resisted a sudden urge to tear up the contract. But he'd wed Lady Rossalyn. And his honor, his pledge, would not be broken.

Malcolm nodded to his men who'd accompanied him to the study. They left to ready for the journey home. Nary one of Gordon's men bade them good travels. If they were in an alliance, each man would rely on another. A brotherhood and its camaraderie was imperative, especially when on patrol. The morale of the Gordon clan had best not be the death of any Sutherland. Malcolm trusted and would give his life for the clan. And they'd do the same for him.

But he kenned in his gut Gordon's men would not, damn them.

Aye, he'd made the deal with the devil, to be sure.

We'll leave as soon as you're ready, her husband had said.

Rossalyn raced to her chamber, more than ready to depart

the keep and her life here. She had no one to say goodbye to, no friend to miss, or family since her mother had died five years ago. Not that it mattered; she was going to a better place and leaving behind the wretched memories of her past.

Liddy was in her chamber, straightening what was already straightened. The keep might lay in shambles, but her chamber was a sanctuary and she did what she could to ensure it was clean and not befouled by the rest.

The kitchen maid blanched and looked to the floor. Rossalyn stopped and fisted her hands at her waist. "You knew? Dear God Almighty, why didn't you warn me?"

Why wasn't she cautioned about the handsome man she'd been set to marry? About his blue eyes and broad shoulders? Her father had told her she was to wed just moments before he ordered her to the main hall. She'd balked, of course, but the man was bound and determined to make the alliance and be rid of her. And Rossalyn kenned such an alliance could very well be the answer to her prayers.

The maid twisted her hands. "I had no choice, m'lady. Yer father warned me not to." When her shoulders trembled, Rossalyn sighed.

"I ken." And she did. Her father knew how to get others to do what he wanted, to be sure. He'd likely threatened Liddy, along with her husband or son. And Liddy now stood quivering as if she feared her own shadow. Poor thing.

A bit of guilt assailed Rossalyn even as she rejoiced at leaving the keep. There were others who deserved a chance of a better life. And while the clan was well fed and filled with drink, their existence seemed so bleak to her.

She looked at the gown she wore and would wear on their trip. The blue was her best gown. 'Twas her wedding gown not only to Laird Sutherland, but to her Daniel as well. She shook her head to stop the memories of her marriage. Although four years had passed, the pain over losing her husband had just started to lessen. All she wanted was to slip on trews and an old liene, rid herself of the memories of auld and new. Then she'd sneak out the rear of the keep and hide within the dense forest, mayhap hunt for a grouse or two.

"My lady."

She lifted a brow.

"Shall I help you pack?" Liddy asked.

"Nay," she said as she caught her reflection in the looking glass. It had been many months since she'd bothered with her appearance. But her curly black hair shone and her cheeks were pink with anticipation. She touched the flushed skin and stared for a moment. She blamed the kiss and the . . . the possessive embrace of her husband.

Clearing her thoughts of the stranger who was now her laird, Rossalyn began gathering her few belongings.

"You may go, Liddy. And be well."

Liddy curtsied. "Best wishes to ye, m'lady."

A knock interrupted the packing and she bade entry.

"Yer ready to leave?" her father questioned with a hard glint in his eyes.

She nodded and began folding clothing to shove into a bag. 'Twasn't much, but she cared not.

"She'll no' be going with ye."

Rossalyn stilled. Had the man had lost his mind?

Sorcha, wife of the clan's smithy, entered, holding wee Mairi's hand.

Her heart raced as rage tore through her body. "Nay, my daughter comes with me."

Her father nodded to Sorcha and she turned to leave.

Rossalyn raced toward them. Her father grabbed her, held her tight against him no matter how hard she struggled.

"Nay, she is mine!" What was she to do? Her daughter, her lovely daughter. She'd never leave her behind.

"She stays. The laird will nae accept another mon's whelp. I swore ye were a maiden."

Why did he vow such an untruth? Laird Sutherland would find out soon enough her father had made an alliance built upon lies. Tears raced down her face and clogged the back of her throat as panic gripped her. "I won't leave."

Her bones nearly cracked as he squeezed her arm. "I need the warriors more than I need to please ye. *Haud yer wheesh*."

"Nay, I'll not be quiet," she cried. "Mairi's my daughter."

He shoved her against the wall, sneered in her face. "I'll no' have a woman telling me what to do. I'm laird and ye'll do as I say."

Taken aback at the vehemence of his words, she tried to nod in agreement. Instead, her ire pushed her to counter, "You've taken all from me. You killed my husband. And now my daughter!"

"If he weren't such a weak man, he'd have killed me instead." Her father laughed, a sickening mix of a cackle and evil chuckle. "And now yer daughter will be raised by Sorcha. 'Tis what she deserves."

Rossalyn gripped his shirt with all the strength she possessed. "You cannot do this to me." The words scratched the back of her throat as tears burned her eyes. She'd not lose another she loved.

Her father lifted his hand and started to bring it against her cheek. As if thinking better of it, he let his arm drop to his side. "Don't want to be giving Laird Sutherland any reason to leave ye behind."

He exited the room and before he strode the hall, Rossalyn heard him sneer, "Let the bairn say her goodbyes."

When his footfalls no longer echoed, Rossalyn frantically searched for her mother's jewels. She gripped the only item remaining from her dowry, since her father had demanded she return the other pieces to him, stating he might marry again one day and would need the gems for his new wife.

Doubtful anyone would wed him or willingly live with him in the keep, nonetheless Rossalyn's fear forced her to comply at her father's insistence. Now she held tight to the last piece of her mother's jewelry. The necklace was worth more than Sorcha had ever seen. And Rossalyn would barter her life if it would save her daughter.

"Quickly," she said to the woman. "Take this." She shoved the necklace toward her and gathered Mairi into her arms. "Ah, my love. We'll be leaving."

Sorcha started to speak. But Rossalyn's harsh glare stopped her. "I am taking my daughter. You will never tell my father. The necklace is to pay for your silence."

Fear and uncertainty shadowed the woman's eyes, but she nodded.

The laird would never be the wiser—fool that he was, he barely ventured from the main hall, much less visited Sorcha's crofter. And if he did? They'd be safe with Laird Sutherland. Surely, her husband would protect them.

Rossalyn gathered herself and whispered to her daughter, "Let us meet where we play games every morning."

Och, it broke her heart when her daughter smiled and skipped out of the chamber. 'Twas truly a hiding place for when her father's rage sought anything or anyone to wreak havoc upon.

She rubbed the back of her neck as she glanced about the chamber. There was nothing left—all of her possessions, and Mairi's things, were packed in a few small bags. The single remaining token of a familial memory had just been given to Sorcha.

After this day, she might never see her father again, thank the Lord. But had she traded one tyrant for another? She pinched the bridge of her nose as she tried to think. Was he a just man? Did he treat women with kindness or as her father had? And did the man like children? As the laird of a keep, he'd need to have children to ensure the line. But many men, those like her father, did as they pleased and treated their children horribly. Tears filled her eyes as she worried about not only her future, but that of her wee Mairi.

Och, she kenned nothing of Laird Sutherland.

She only knew his kisses caused warmth to curl from her head to her toes. And when he finally explored her body, she would not be frightened. Nay, she would welcome his touch. She would want it.

And oh, how she needed it.

Laird Sutherland seemed equally enthralled with her, but men weren't as picky with their companions as women were. And if he had a need for the alliance, he'd have most likely married anyone.

When he found out he'd been tricked? Dear God, she prayed they wouldn't feel the brunt of his wrath.

Chapter 3

"Ready the wagons and horses," Malcolm instructed his men. By his reckoning they'd be on their way within the hour.

He glanced up at the keep. Someone spied on him and he'd bet 'twas Laird Gordon. The situation was unsettling. Yet, 'twas too late to change his dealings with the devil. In the future, he'd send his steward to complete any transactions or secure forces. His steward and several men for protection.

"M'laird?"

He turned toward the soft voice and grinned. Aye, the deal with the devil may have been worth it. Foolish to think he could ken a woman in such a short time, but the kindness in her eyes and the way she kissed him spoke to him. Triggered a warmth in the pit of his gut he felt he could trust. Such a sweet lady didn't deserve to remain at the keep with these sorts of men.

For a moment, he worried she might be like her father. He searched her face, her eyes for any sign of duplicity. Then she smiled. 'Twas like sunshine itself on a dreary day.

He had few demands of a wife. But one he wasn't willing to negotiate on was a chaste wife. After his fiancée Trina had betrayed him, 'twas the only thing that mattered. And not only Laird Gordon, but the doctor himself had sworn she was pure. Gordon's word was suspect, but the doctor? He'd been willing to swear upon the word of God.

As he looked at her, enchanting and lovely, Malcolm was convinced he'd made the right choice, his distrust of her father be damned. She tipped her head to the side and he realized he hadn't spoken, but had rudely stared at her.

"Aye," he finally said.

"Will I travel in a wagon or on horseback?"

She bit at her lip and kept looking over her shoulder. 'Twas obvious she wanted to quit the keep as quickly as he did.

"A covered wagon, to be sure. You'll have one to yourself. The trip will be long and hard." He reached for her and rubbed his hand along her arm. He couldn't help himself—he wanted to touch her over and over again.

She glanced nervously toward the keep once more.

He furrowed his brow. "Or would you prefer a horse?"

"Nay," his wife said with a quick shake of her head. "The wagon will suit."

She smiled at him. Och, if he could have her smile at him like that for the rest of his life, 'twould be worth it.

Damn, her lips distracted him and he leaned down. Just one, he promised. She moved toward him, anticipating his actions. They met in the middle, their bodies curved into each other, his hard, hers incredibly soft. Ah, so soft. Her breasts pushed against his chest and he wanted to rid her of clothing and just look, then touch, then suckle until she writhed beneath him.

Rossalyn whimpered when he parted her lips with his tongue. Hot, moist, and welcoming. She'd a bit of passion in her. Pleased at her response to his kiss, he moved toward her once again.

A throat cleared behind him.

Bollocks.

"We're nearly ready, m'laird."

He eased away and without looking replied, "Aye, Cam." Malcolm held onto his wife for just a moment more. "Please tell me if you need anything."

"Aye, m'laird," she answered.

"Interesting," his Sargent-at-Arms stated as his brow quirked upward.

"*Haud yer wheesh*." Malcolm grinned despite himself as he watched her gather her bags and direct his men to load supplies. The graceful way she moved, her confidence when she spoke to his people, all put him at ease. Gordon Keep might rest in shambles, but his lady kenned how to get things done.

"Are you going to mount up or stare at your wife like a lovesick lad?"

He glared at his friend who merely held his hands up and bowed before heading toward his steed.

Soon they'd be home. He'd have a woman in his arms, a lady for his keep and hopefully in the months to come, a bairn to further the Sutherland name.

Rossalyn could barely breathe as she wrapped Mairi in a blanket and snuck her into her wagon. The lass was quiet, as if they were playing a game. She prayed her daughter's presence would remain a secret until they left Gordon lands.

The laird had covered the wagon to protect her from the ever-changing Scottish weather. Aye, he seemed to be a kind man. From a slim opening in the cover, she regarded him as Mairi snuggled in behind her. He led his men firmly, but a smile graced his face more often than not. When there was a need, he heaved supplies or saddled a horse. And when a cow broke free of its tether, he chased the beastie until it was caught and once again secured. She shook her head in disbelief, for the man had laughed the entire time.

Her father, his men—they'd more than likely shoot the cow dead with an arrow before giving chase. 'Twas the type of men they were. She worried the bargain he had made with Laird Sutherland would not come to fruition. Her father was a bastard of a man and rarely kept his pledge. Since she was now leaving, forever out of his way, she kenned he'd never hold up his end of the alliance. He was rid of her, a reminder of her mother and happier times at Gordon Keep. 'Twas some of the reason her father loathed her. And when Mairi was born, his loathing often turned to rage. He wanted everyone as unhappy as he was. Rossalyn had refused to bow to his demands and instead made a life for her little family as if they were living in a different keep with a different laird.

At last they were headed to a better place. But if her father broke his pledge to Laird Sutherland, where would she and Mairi go? For surely her new laird would banish her when her father failed to keep his word. And when he discovered Mairi, he might even do worse.

"Stay hidden, my love," she whispered to her daughter. A bright grin filled Mairi's face. Och, such a sweet lass.

"Are you well, m'lady?"

She started at her husband's voice. "Aye." Her heart pounding against her chest, she moved toward him lest his gaze rest on Mairi. She'd nestled their bags as if they were a little wall between her daughter and the front of the wagon. 'Twas a fool's errand to attempt such a secret. But to keep them safe and away from her father and his lecherous men, she had to try.

Sean, her father's steward, had made comments for the past few months about her mourning period being done, insinuating the laird would expect her to marry—mayhap him, he'd say with a snide grin. Not that she didn't want a man in her life, but 'twas the worry her father would marry her off to one of his men. Och, 'twould be wretched to marry a clansman with missing teeth and a paunch which hung over his tartan.

Yet her father *had* married her off—to a stranger. Which was worse, she wondered, Laird Sutherland or the steward? 'Twas a case of *the devil you ken*, but as she looked at her husband, she suspected the steward would have been the worst option possible.

The laird propped himself against the wagon and she desperately looked for something or someone to distract him away from the bundle near the back. Then he touched her hand. Her gaze seeking his, she moved forward, nearly melting into the kindness she saw reflected in their depths. Surely, he wasn't like the steward?

"I thought I heard you speaking to someone," he said.

Heat flooded her face as she ducked her gaze. "I was speaking to myself."

He chuckled and tipped up her chin. "I've been known to do that as well. Ask my men."

A sense of ease washed over her, something warm and comforting. "How far is your keep?"

"At least five days." As he spoke, he swept his thumb back and forth along her arm. She shivered from the pleasure of it and his cocksure grin told her he'd felt her tremble.

Though she nodded at his answer, dread filled her. The journey's length meant an impossible amount of time to hide her daughter. If her calculations were correct, they'd leave Gordon lands in just over a day or two. Mayhap, if she prayed hard enough, God would keep Mairi safe until she could explain the situation to Laird Sutherland. Consequences be damned, her daughter was her first concern and he'd have to understand her actions.

"Rossalyn."

She closed her eyes. The way he said her name—reverent, with a deep huskiness, left her a little breathless. "Aye," she whispered.

"Look at me."

When she complied, he continued, "I want to assure you that we will celebrate our marriage at my keep."

She furrowed her brow. Did he truly mean that? Och, 'twould be a miracle if he did.

"I do not want you to fear me. We need time to learn each other."

Relief flooded her. Mayhap she'd be able to keep Mairi a secret longer than she thought. She smiled up at him. "You are a good man, Laird Sutherland." She meant the words, and hoped his goodness would remain when he determined her secret.

He offered a wry grin. "Call me Malcolm. You are my wife, no matter if we have yet to be intimate."

Joy filled her and a bit of trust grew for this Highlander. Could her luck be changing? Would it be possible to live her life with an honorable man? Not that Daniel wasn't honorable, but his dealings, the trades he'd made and the way he vexed her father, had made their life tenuous. And when he tried to protect her against her father's wrath, her father had killed him.

Rossalyn's breath hitched. "Thank you." She squeezed his hand.

His gaze softened and tiny wrinkles fanned out from the corners of his eyes. Och, 'twas a handsome trait, those little lines. Malcolm brushed his hand along her cheek. "We have the rest of our lives together."

How sweet those words sounded to her. The rest of their lives. As much as she tried not to, she pinned hope on his words, that such hope might aid her in the days to come.

One of his men called out and it appeared as if the caravan of horses and wagons was ready to leave.

"I will check on you soon." His gaze held hers and the promise of their future lay heady in his brown eyes. He kissed her brow and moved to mount his horse.

She watched him go with an odd sort of longing to be with him, riding beside him as they left Gordon territory together and swept further into Sutherland land. Impossible, she kenned, but something pulled at her regardless.

She climbed into the wagon and after nestling her sleeping daughter toward her, settled in as the creak of the wagon wheels told her they were on the move.

Her gaze lit on Mairi's lovely face. Such a dear child, so sweet and innocent, with the ability to fall asleep within a thrice. Her pert nose wrinkled and she snuggled closer. Rossalyn sighed and gently brushed the child's unruly curls behind her ear. She was Daniel's daughter, to be sure, with his wide eyes that held a twinkle of mischief and his strong cheek and brow.

Och, her heart ached at the memories of her husband. And how her father had reacted when Daniel questioned the laird's treatment of her. She'd begged him. Begged him to stop fighting. She'd witnessed her father's wrath too many times to count and it was always harsh and swift.

But Daniel wanted to protect her . . . them. 'Twas his duty, he'd vowed, when he reached for his sword and her father had grabbed for his.

How Daniel had been goaded into making the first move! He had parried, but her father was an expert swordsman and her dear husband was not. The men of the clan cheered the fight and were no help in stopping it. Wagers were set, drinks raised. *The bastards.*

And when he'd cleaved her husband in two, her father had lived up to his ruthless reputation. Worse, he accepted congratulations from the clansmen as Daniel lay bleeding in the middle of the main hall.

She had tried to use her skirt to stop the blood flow, to no avail. Her husband was gone. Forever gone, cut down by his own laird without a second thought. Her father cared naught of Daniel's life and hers, or—most importantly—that of his granddaughter's.

The memories wrought tears of frustration. She swiped at them, whisked them away as she tried to look forward to leaving the troublesome past of Gordon Keep behind her.

She peered out the back of the wagon as her childhood home became smaller and smaller. Despite the wretched memories, new hope settled in and took root in her heart.

"I'll make sure your life is better, my love. I promise."

Aye, she owed it to her daughter and the memory of her dead husband.

Chapter 4

The night sky nearly spilled over with twinkling stars, the very air quiet, save the rustle of dry leaves still hanging on for dear life in the burgeoning winter weather.

Rossalyn peeked from her wagon to assure all were abed and thus safe for her to bring Mairi to the small creek burbling nearby. 'Twas a difficult task keeping such a wee lass quiet and hidden when her daughter was full of babble about their adventure and yearned to join the men near the fire.

She had to promise great things to her daughter when they reached the keep, and could only hope they had a grand supply of ponies and sweets.

"Shhh, my love," she warned. She tucked the child within the material of her gown and they snuck through the small thicket of trees surround the camp. Ah, the water called to her no matter its frigid state. They were used to rustic accommodations, but had enjoyed bathing nearly every day, even if Rossalyn had to cart the water herself. And it had been several days since they'd left the keep.

"Mother, can I swim?"

She smiled despite her rattled nerves. "Nay, my love, but we can quickly bathe."

"I hate baths."

Aye, 'twas the truth of it. The lass often balked when she had to bathe. "When we reach the keep, I promise you we will have the most delicious sweets you can imagine."

Mairi squeezed her hand. "With honey?"

She ruffled her daughter's hair. "Aye, with honey."

"M'lady?"

She closed her eyes and sighed, then quickly pulled her gown tighter around Mairi. How did she expect Laird Sutherland not to have men patrolling the area? If she wasn't careful, he'd learn of her daughter and Rossalyn would have to plead with him to not send them back.

She held her finger to her lips to silence Mairi. "I'm bathing."

The steps quickly retreated. "Sorry I am, m'lady."

They finished quickly and she kept Mairi partially behind her as she walked. Before they entered the camp, a quick look told her the guard was nowhere to be seen. After she sighed with relief, they snuck back into the wagon.

She spoke softly to her daughter and the child fell asleep within a thrice. Not used to sitting all day in a wagon, Rossalyn went to warm herself by the fire on the opposite side of the camp.

"You could not sleep?"

For a man his size, he certainly moved quietly. "Nay," she said to her husband.

He sat beside her and held out a tumbler. She took a sip of ale, relishing the drink as it filled her stomach. Her father's steward had let the ale spoil more times than not and she'd taken to drinking freshly drawn milk or water from the well. No matter how many times she asked her father if she could oversee the kitchen and the ale, he refused and would send her back to her chamber. 'Twas as if he preferred to live within the punishing squalor.

He nodded toward her wagon. "The guard said you bathed in the creek?"

'Twas more of a statement than a question. "Aye."

He stared at her, his brow furrowed. "'Tisn't safe. Next time tell me and I'll ensure naught happens to you."

She tilted her head to the side as she regarded him. It had been so long since someone had wanted to protect her. Too long. "I assure you I was very safe."

His frown deepened. "I protect what is mine."

Rossalyn waited a moment, thinking she wasn't going to win this argument. But this would make things with Mairi much more difficult. She was torn. She loved how he wanted to protect her, but loathed having to be guarded for her every movement while she attempted to keep her secret. Och, 'twas an impossible feat, keeping her daughter hidden. "Aye, m'laird."

He nodded and a pleased smile curled his lips. "You will have my mother's chamber when we return. You will enjoy her room."

She drew her brows upward. "Where will she go?"

He looked toward the fire, then said, "My mother died last year and my father shortly after." His voice roughened, tensed. His jaw clenched as his gaze held on the flames of the burning fire. She kenned her husband's thoughts bittersweet as he remembered his parents, their time together and sadly, their death.

She touched his arm, her heart aching at his pain. There was so much to learn about the man. "I'm so sorry."

His shoulders had stiffened. "'Twas an illness that felled many of the elder clansmen." He tossed another log onto the fire.

The warmth from the flames felt as comforting as his arms when he pulled her closer and protected her from the force of the buffeting wind.

"I lost my mother as well." She shuddered at the thought, the death of her mother still as fresh as if it happened the eve before. "I miss her keenly."

"Aye." He kissed the top of her head and she resisted the urge to pull away.

Such intimacy was unfamiliar to her, not unwelcome, but unaccustomed. And even as she craved a man's caress, she'd been so long without compassion and desire, she still startled a bit at his touch. Here was a man she barely kenned, even though she was drawn to him more than her initial attraction to Daniel. When she was near Malcolm, her belly heated and her heart longed for a grin or even his gaze to seek hers.

This seemed too fast and fiery, when her marriage to Daniel had been a slow courtship. While she loved him, she kenned they didn't share a consuming passion for each other. He was her friend and confidant, and then her husband and lover. When Mairi was born they grew closer, mayhap due to the need to protect her, since together they were stronger.

Now she whispered, "After my mother passed on Christmas Eve, my father changed. He's . . . he's been a wretched man since." And she had lived in fear for her family's life since that fateful day. Especially once Daniel had died. There was no one to champion them and stand up to her father. No one to ensure they had fresh meat and other food stores. 'Twas why she started hunting for rabbit or grouse when possible.

Och, food stores. She should tell Malcolm her father was untrustworthy, but by the way he'd spoken to her father and his men, Laird Sutherland might already ken exactly who her father was. And if anyone could force Laird Gordon to keep his end of the bargain, somehow she knew 'twas her husband and his men.

Before her mother's death, they'd celebrated Christmas with food, dancing, and gifts. Och, the Yule log was so large, it would burn for days. And she'd giggled when she witnessed couples kissing beneath the large mistletoe balls.

Her mother and father would observe the clan, pride shining on their faces. They provided gifts to all, small trinkets and shortbread, but so appreciated by everyone.

'Twas some of her fondest memories, some of the only memories which had kept her sane after her mother's and Daniel's deaths. Dear God Almighty, she'd held onto them, wrapped those memories around her, and tried to not allow her father to ruin her life.

Her reverie was interrupted when some of Malcolm's men approached to warm by the fire. He stood and she shivered. Should she tell him she wanted him beside her? Or would her boldness embarrass him before his men? 'Twas hard to think when she didn't ken well enough to discern his moods, likes, and dislikes.

"Sorry, m'laird. We didnae ken the lady was awake."

She glanced to the ground. Now she was embarrassed. "I'll take my leave."

He held out his hand and grinned. "I will escort you."

She worried her lip. Dare she say no? And if she did, wouldn't he suspect her behavior?

"M'laird! 'Tis a rider approaching."

She sighed with relief. Her secret would keep for another night.

Malcolm stiffened and she felt the strain of his muscles as if they turned to stone. He glanced at her and his jaw clenched. She nodded to give him leave. He squeezed her hand and bade one of his men to look after her. Taking up his sword, with a few strong strides he was away from the camp and heading toward an unknown danger.

A pang, of worry and fear, clenched her chest as he disappeared through the trees.

"M'lady," Malcolm's man said, "'twould be better for ye in the wagon."

Aye, she knew her daughter was safe, but what of her new laird? Would the fates be so cruel as to steal another husband from her? She prayed for Malcolm's safety, begged the dear Lord to bring him back to her and in that fleeting moment, she promised to tell him the truth, no matter the cost.

'Twas only a farmer looking for his sheep.

Malcolm swiped at the back of his neck. If he never set foot off Sutherland land again, 'twould be too soon. When he'd heard that a rider approached, he wondered if Gordon had sent men to fetch Rossalyn back.

His gut dropped. He vowed never to let her go, and damned if he didn't want to rush back to camp just to gaze upon her and listen to her speak. Her voice seemed to entwine with his thoughts, hypnotizing him. Soft in tone, but husky.

And it fascinated as well as plagued him.

How could a woman capture his attention so completely in such a short time? Especially since he'd been determined to marry because he must, but his heart—well, 'twas his alone. The marriage would be one of necessity. They'd find comfort with each other, for their attraction was obvious and he would be a faithful and kind husband; a provider for their bairns if they were so blessed.

But she'd never have his heart.

He had pledged it as so.

His honor was at stake. If he allowed another woman to trifle with his heart, love him and then scorn him, his men wouldn't respect him. His *clan* wouldn't respect him. And he'd rather die than lose the respect of the Sutherlands.

"M'Laird," Cam said with a slightly mocking tone, as if he knew what Malcolm was thinking and pitied him for it.

"Let's return to the camp. We've a long ride ahead of us."

His man hesitated, then fell into step beside him. "Aye, m'laird."

Malcolm nearly rolled his eyes as he stopped walking and settled his fists on his hips. "Speak your mind."

Cam chuckled. "She's a beauty, to be sure."

'Twas his turn to grin. The most beautiful woman he'd ever seen with her dark as night hair and those clear, sapphire eyes. "Aye."

"A sweet lass," Cam said with a shrug. "Despite the bastard of a father."

Malcolm dragged his fingers through his hair. The clan depended on him to ensure not only their safety, but their well-being. They needed a lady who'd care for them, keep them strong, and keep him in line. And he'd promised himself a Christmas bride.

Nowhere in the prospect of finding a bride did he think there'd be a mutual attraction and respect; a growing emotion. *Not to mention my aching cock.* But his former betrothed had forsaken him and run away, thus affecting the security of his own decisions. 'Twas excellent Cam could see the goodness in Lady Rossalyn as well. Malcolm trusted the man with his life and that of the clan. To hear him say the words eased some of his uncertainty.

But he had to keep a clear mind, not one befuddled with a comely lass, despite the fact she was his wife.

Malcolm steeled himself as he paced toward the camp, a demand for his heart and mind not to be captivated by his wife.

His clan and sanity depended on it.

Chapter 5

The wagon rolled and pitched as they climbed higher into the Highlands. Would they ever reach their destination? 'Twas getting harder and harder to keep Mairi hidden. Each night they'd sneak out to find fresh water or stretch their legs. If there were no riders behind the wagon, she'd let Mairi stand and move about. But, 'twas not often the wagon wasn't surrounded by her husband's men.

Surprisingly, her father had chosen the Sutherland clan wisely. The men were well trained and serious in their duty to their laird. Loyalty was obvious as was their affection for her husband. Many a time she heard their discussions as they traveled. When the clansmen spoke of him reverently, pride straightened their spines and broadened their shoulders.

Such a change from the Gordon men, who were more likely to fight each other than support the clan.

Laird Sutherland continued to seek her company, but he'd appeared more aloof. Reserved. She searched her mind wondering if she'd offended him, but she could think of nothing. Mayhap it was better this way, maintaining a distance from her husband and keeping her secret a little longer. At least until they reached Sutherland Keep and she could explain why her father had deceived him, and her own complicity in not coming forward with the truth.

Since a persistent drizzle had kept her to the protection of the wagon, she'd become nearly as restless as Mairi. Sutherland's men brought her food, allowed her a few moments of privacy, but quickly secured her back in the wagon before moving northward.

"When shall we arrive at the keep?"

She smiled at her daughter. "Soon, I wager. And then," she said as she kissed Mairi's sweet nose, "you shall enjoy yourself every single day, my love."

A twinkle flashed in Mairi's eyes. "Then I shall have sweets to break my fast and a pony to ride."

Rossalyn laughed. Och, she'd promised too much!

"Tell me a story," Mairi begged. Rossalyn nearly refused, but the lass had been so good, she deserved whatever she asked for.

"What type of story?"

Mairi scrunched her nose as she thought. Och, she looked so much like Daniel. "Tell me about Christmas."

The poor lass hadn't celebrated Christmas, but had heard Rossalyn speak of past celebrations. Her curiosity was never sated, no matter how many times Rossalyn told the stories.

"Hmmm. My first Christmas with your father was so lovely. He'd been hunting and brought home a large buck. Cook made every dish imaginable and the sweets—so delicious. Och, the tree was lit with so many candles I was nearly blinded. But 'twas much more special because of you."

Her daughter's brow quirked. "Me?"

"Aye," Rossalyn said as she tweaked her nose. "I kenned you were growing in my belly." She patted her stomach. "We were so happy."

Daniel had shouted throughout the entire keep when she told him. Many a toast was raised that evening, their first Christmas and a bairn. Her mother and father were so pleased. They'd smiled and laughed, even danced a bit. Aye, 'twas a wonderful memory and a wonderful time of year filled with dancing and merriment, the love of a good man and a bairn on the way. 'Twas special, but those special moments were gone too soon.

That evening, her mother had gone to sleep and never woke. Tragic and devastating was their loss.

Both Rossalyn and her father were never the same—but her father—och, he'd become the devil. Full of drink and belligerence. More often than not, he'd strike against anyone for a look or misspoken word. The keep went to ruin and the people were either too frightened or too quarrelsome to protest or take matters into their own hands.

Aye, and a few months after Mairi was born, her father had raged against her for the spoiled ale. Daniel had come to her defense. Rossalyn often wondered why she'd caught the blame when the steward was the only one allowed in the buttery and oversaw the ale.

Then had come the dawning. He couldn't stand her happiness. His wife was dead. And Rossalyn didn't have the right to be happily wed. Every smile and hoot of laughter was like a stab in his eye. 'Twas why he provoked the argument because he kenned Daniel would fight him, especially when her father tried to raise his hand to her.

If only she could have foreseen his plan, sensed his temper that eve. Then Daniel would be alive and well. They'd still be a family.

She brushed away the sadness, and tucked Mairi against the back of the wagon, pulling a blanket tight about her chin. "Now sleep, my love."

"M'lady?"

Her heart sank to her stomach as she furtively glanced between her daughter and the edge of the wagon covering, where Malcolm stood. "Aye," she said as she turned and held her finger to her lips, scooting Mairi further beneath the blanket.

"Remember our game, my love." She winked at her daughter and left the wagon.

"We'll arrive before nightfall," he stated.

Startled, she glanced toward the mountain before her and saw traces of smoke far in the distance, the stone walls of a keep.

Their new home. Sutherland Keep.

"When we arrive, I will introduce you." He followed her gaze, though a deep furrow pinched his brow. "I expect you to care for my people."

Her eyes widened. Did he think she didn't ken what it meant to be lady of the keep? "Aye, m'laird." She thought a moment. Of course he'd question her capabilities after he'd seen her home and its state.

"And," he said with a low growl, "we'll celebrate Christmas."

If possible her heart beat faster against her chest. Hope surged and she could barely catch her breath.

Christmas.

Tears blurred her vision. How excited Mairi would be.

She quickly envisioned a keep filled with mistletoe, pine, and food. Och, the meals they'd enjoy—and dancing, 'twould be merry dancing for all. She'd ensure a special time for the clan as their new lady and most especially for her wee daughter.

He tipped up her chin and she couldn't tell if his scowl was because he was vexed or confused. "I do not mean to make you sad."

She shook her head and covered his hands with her own. "Nay, m'laird. I am so pleased."

His scowl deepened. "Pleased?"

"Aye." She leaned up and kissed his cheek. She lingered, enthralled with his generosity and the scent of leather and male. He placed his hand at the small of her back, bracing her against him.

A rider approached, spewing up dirt and rocks as the horse barreled down the pathway. The closer the rider came, Rossalyn realized 'twas a woman. Her hair flew behind her with abandon and her *arisaid* waved in the wind like a flapping sail.

Her husband grinned, then pulled away and walked toward the woman.

"Malcolm," the woman called as she quickly dismounted. "We've been waiting for ages. Did you secure the needed supplies?"

Malcolm turned to the woman and threw his head back, laughing. Rossalyn gripped her chest at the sound coming from him. Why, 'twas merry, jovial, and incredibly attractive. She found herself smiling along with him.

"I see you couldn't wait for us, impatient lass."

The lovely woman ran to Malcolm and jumped into his arms. "I couldn't wait to see *you*."

There was something in her tone that alerted Rossalyn to move forward and gain the woman's attention.

"And who is this? Some woman you found wandering the Highlands in need of rescue?" There was nothing friendly in her tone; nay, a direct warning laced her words.

"*Fiona*." Malcolm removed her arms from around his neck. "I did secure the goods we needed and will continue to need."

He'd obviously kept the details of the alliance from his clan.

The woman pouted and Rossalyn wanted to slap her. Mostly because this Fiona was truly one of the most beautiful women she'd ever seen. Long red hair curled over her shoulders and down her back. And Fiona possessed a figure Rossalyn knew men lusted after—full breasts, impossibly small waist.

Piercing green eyes directed hatred in Rossalyn's direction. She smoothed a hand over her skirt, knowing she looked like a wretch.

"Who is she, Malcolm?" Fiona paced toward her and looked down her nose. "She could do with a bath."

Rossalyn squared her shoulders. How dare the woman talk to her with such disrespect?

"Fiona," Malcolm growled. "You will not speak to my lady in such a manner."

An ugly sneer contorted the woman's face. Rossalyn straightened and attempted a haughty mien, despite the chill racing up her spine.

"*Your what*?"

Malcolm came to Rossalyn's side and pulled her to him. "Lady Rossalyn and I were wed before I left Gordon Keep." His arm steadied her and she was thankful for his support.

"How could you?" Fiona screeched as she lunged for him. "We were to wed. We were promised."

"Enough," Cam yelled as he paced toward them. "*Haud yer wheesh*." He gripped Fiona's arm and dragged her away, forcing her to mount her horse. When he returned, he bowed to Rossalyn. "Please forgive her, m'lady. She knows not what she says."

She offered a smile and nodded. "Please do not worry, Cam."

He played the rogue and winked at her. "Thank you, m'lady." Then he was off, presumably to ensure the lass did as she was told.

"That was very gracious of you." Malcolm turned her toward him, his brows pinched and his gaze intense. "What to make of you? One moment I want to ravish you and the next, I want to send you back to your bastard of a father."

"I prefer the first, rather than the latter." She offered a hesitant smile, then realized what she had said. "M'laird, I did not mean—"

He held up a hand as a quick grin lifted his mouth. He brushed the hair from his brow. "Fiona—" he started.

"Aye, I believe she is enamored with you." Rossalyn tried to keep the mood light, for she liked the smile playing on his mouth and the softness of his gaze. And his touch left her a bit breathless.

"She believes a childhood pledge between a lad and a lass." With a rueful frown, he shook his head. "Any other time, such a pledge might be honored, but the promise of a boy of only nine summers cannot be taken seriously. We've never been able to convince her otherwise."

"No matter." She released a held breath and dared to look into his eyes. His brows had lowered as if he were warring with himself. Then slowly, torturously, he moved toward her until he plundered her lips in a kiss.

Dear God Almighty, would she ever get used to the hot surge of desire racing through her body at his touch?

Malcolm teased and nipped, tasted and licked. Heat pooled deep within her womb and she ached for him. 'Twas a wonderful and frightening feeling, the power this man held over her with just a kiss.

She moaned as he kissed along her jaw, nuzzled at the sensitive spot just below her ear. His hot breath fanned along her skin, tantalizing. So . . . so . . . *incredible*. She gripped his shoulders, gaining purchase in his broad muscles, lest she weaken and fall.

"Beautiful," he whispered along his trail of kisses. "So lovely."

She smiled, loving his mouth along her skin.

"Mother?"

Chapter 6

Malcolm tore himself from Rossalyn and turned toward the soft voice of a child.

"Mairi, no," his wife wailed.

The lass is hers?

The child ran toward Rossalyn, burying her face against her bosom. Tears raced down Rossalyn's cheeks as her mouth contorted as if in pain. "Please," she begged, "you must understand."

Anger unfurled, slowly, but potently.

He was fooled. Again.

"She is yours, no?" he ground out.

More tears fell and her chin trembled.

He didn't give a damn.

"*She is yours*?"

She nodded and gripped her daughter closer. The lass looked at him with fear in her big eyes as she clung to her mother.

"And her father?"

Were they even legally wed?

She glanced up at him. "He's dead."

At least she hadn't completely humiliated him with this deception. "Cam!" he bellowed. "We return to the Gordon Keep."

"Nay," Rossalyn cried. She gently moved her daughter behind her. "Nay!"

He rested his fists on his hips and glared at her. "You dare tell me nay?" The woman was daft. "You have *lied* to me."

She gripped his shirt. "Please do not make us go," she

pleaded.

He pushed her away. "I was promised a chaste wife." His gaze cut to the lass. "And you are not. Who kens what else you have lied about?" Deceit plagued him—tore at his soul. First with the woman he was going to marry and now with the woman he had wed.

She fell into a heap before him, her shoulders shaking as she sobbed.

Cam arrived and took in the scene before him. "M'laird?" His man's discomfort was obvious as he tried not to look at Rossalyn and Mairi, but his gaze shifted between them in confusion.

"We will return to Gordon Keep."

He sputtered. "M'laird, the men are weary—the horses need to rest." Cam leaned closer. "Your wife needs the comfort of the keep."

Malcolm didn't give a damn what his wife needed. He would be rid of her.

She had deceived him.

Cam gripped his shoulder. Malcolm glared at his Sargent-at-Arms, a man he trusted.

"Think of the lass, Malcolm." He removed his hand when Malcolm growled. "She's a wee thing and would surely perish if we do not allow her to rest."

Malcolm sighed and looked to the heavens for guidance. As if God were listening, snow began to fall; slowly, but 'twas snow. He spared the lass a glance and she stared at him with those wide eyes of hers. Pools of tears settled within them and one slipped over her lashes.

Bollocks.

"Proceed to the keep," he said in a low growl. Then he'd deal with his wife and her child. Even if it meant resting before heading back to Gordon on the morrow.

"M'laird." Rossalyn swiped at the tears treading down her face. "Thank you."

He looked down his nose at her. He'd been swayed by her beauty. Anger clenched his muscles. "Your fate is yet to be determined, m'lady."

She faltered as she tried to lead her daughter back to the wagon. The lass kept her gaze pinned on him and damned if he didn't feel as if he were a monster. Malcolm swept his hand through his hair and released a rough sigh.

He didn't deal in untruths. He would never trick someone into a marriage under false pretense. How had he managed to choose two women who'd deceived him?

"Don't let her leave the wagon," he ordered Cam.

Cam nodded, but Malcolm felt his censure. No matter. He was laird of the Sutherlands. Not Cam, not his wife. He would make the decisions and mete out the punishments.

Cam came toward him. "Do not judge her too harshly, m'laird."

"They both lied," he growled.

His man sighed and watched Rossalyn gently guide Mairi toward the wagon. "You saw Gordon, his men—the keep. A gentlewoman should never have to live amongst that filth."

"No matter." Malcolm cut his hand through the air. "The laird and priest swore she was chaste."

Cam cursed beneath his breath. "Did you ask her why? Perhaps she didn't lie at all."

He snapped his gaze to Cam. "Come on, man. Why would she hide the lass if she didn't ken what Gordon had promised?"

"She is not Trina, Malcolm."

"How dare you judge me? She lied, the same as Trina."

And as soon as he could, he'd rid himself of his wife, to be sure.

"Don't cry, Mother."

Rossalyn pulled her daughter close and snuggled against

her soft, curly hair. Och, Mairi was her heart. If they returned to Gordon Keep, her father would bring his wrath upon them. She cared not for herself, but Mairi . . .

"Do not worry for me, my love." She kissed Mairi's brow and pulled a blanket over them. Soon they'd arrive at the Sutherland Keep and their fate would await them.

Surely the people would shun her if her husband shared her deceit. Would he? Of course he would. He'd said he was going to return her to Gordon land. If Cam hadn't stepped in, they'd be on their way back to hell. Time would only tell how her husband was going to punish her.

Shouts in the distance assured they were near.

Near to the keep, and her destiny.

Mairi gripped her hand as she was wont to do when she slept. Such dreams she had for her child. Even after Daniel was slain, Rossalyn always pushed for a better life for her dear lass. Hiding her from the evilness of the clan, the utter filth that seemed to cloak the keep and the minds of the men inside. Aye, they'd stayed cloistered in her chamber as much as possible. But they'd been safe.

Until Laird Malcolm Sutherland had arrived and offered her a ray of hope, a promise of a better future, the lovely idea of celebrating Christmas. Tears blurred her vision and she wiped at them. They didn't need much, nay, they just needed to be safe.

And for wee Mairi, a Christmas celebration she'd never forget, whether she be on Sutherland soil or banished to Gordon Keep.

"Wife," a voice growled outside the wagon.

She held back a sigh, in no condition to spar with the man who confused her so. One moment he held her in his arms and her blood surged with longing, desire. The next he turned cold as mountain stone. All because she'd omitted to tell him. Och, how she regretted her actions. Why hadn't she done so before they left the keep?

Simply, because she feared he'd refuse her and make her remain with her father.

When her gaze met his, the icy glare had her gripping her daughter and freezing in place.

"I'd like to speak to you, wife," he demanded.

Dear Lord, the way he said *wife* was as if he called to the devil. Mairi moved restlessly as if she'd heard the laird speak, but blessedly remained asleep.

Rossalyn scooted to the end of the wagon and the laird held out a hand to help her exit. She jerked when their hands touched.

"We will arrive and you will take your place at my side."

Her heart raced. Had he forgiven her? Did she dare hope God had answered her prayers?

"Thank you," she whispered as tears clogged her throat. "I can't tell you—"

He held up his palm to stop her from speaking. His jaw clenched and a foreboding scowl turned down his mouth. "Do not thank me. I am not doing this for you, but for my clan."

Rossalyn shrank back. *For his clan.*

Aye, she imagined 'twas his first consideration. But a small part of her wished he were doing it for them. Foolish, but her hope had been the only thing she could cling to, it had helped her keep Mairi quiet, and set her mind on their future at Sutherland Keep.

"I vow," he said in a low, husky rumble, "if I learn of any more deceit, I'll return you to your father. We are wed, but 'tis all. I will not seek your counsel *or* your bed."

She glanced up at him in surprise. Her worst fears were realized, for now she'd be living with a man who loathed her, just as her father had. Laird Sutherland peered at her with a heavy dose of disdain when just a few hours ago he had gazed upon her with desire.

He'd not shaven in several days and his beard's growth darkened the edge of his strong jaw. Dangerous and incredibly handsome, his eyes darkened to nearly black. As he stepped aside, his kilt swayed, revealing legs thick with muscle.

The Gordon men were lazy, more apt to pick up a tumbler of ale than a practice sword. 'Twas part of the reason her father needed the alliance with Sutherland.

And the man hated her, 'twas obvious in his gaze and his words.

With one last glance, he strode to his steed.

Chilled, she rubbed her hands along her arms.

He never looked back. Her spirit broke along with her heart.

They rode into the keep amid grand applause. She peeked out of the wagon as clansmen cheered their laird's arrival.

The keep rose from the mountain as if it were a mighty oak sprouting from stone. The palisade gate was open and the travelers entered. As the wagon stopped, she moved to gather their meager belongings.

Cam helped her and Mairi exit the wagon. He avoided her gaze and she was thankful for it. "A maid will show you to your chamber. M'laird said you needn't join him for the evening meal."

Taken aback, she sought Malcolm's tall form. He spared her a glance then continued talking to those gathered around him. She assumed the clansmen would be curious about her. Surely, the redheaded woman had spread word of her arrival. Such a large clan with men and women of all ages, they smiled and laughed, obviously pleased their laird had arrived back home safely.

'Twas utterly shameful he didn't introduce her immediately. Flustered, she nodded to Cam. 'Twould not bode well to disregard her husband's edict by going to the evening meal. However, she wanted to make an impression on the clan and assure them she would be a good lady of the keep. "We're ready to see our chamber," she said with her chin up and a straight back. She gripped Mairi's hand and squeezed.

Her daughter looked up at her with solemn eyes. Fear trembled her lips. 'Twas what Rossalyn worried would happen. Just when she was trying to do the best for them, the circumstances changed and now they were being treated exactly the way she had feared.

Cam nodded. His cheeks flushed red and his throat bobbed as if he were thinking of something to say. Aye, well, at least she wasn't the only one embarrassed by the laird's actions.

He guided them toward the main entrance of the keep and said, "M'laird will see you in the morn."

She stared at the broad doors before them. Somewhere behind those doors was her new home. A chamber for her and Mairi, a main hall, more rooms; a kitchen. A true home she wanted to embrace.

"Aye," she barely managed before she was forced to swallow back tears. The clan must think her a horrid lady, to be sure. She paused and looked over her shoulder at the growing crowd of clansmen surrounding Laird Sutherland. Should she ignore his wishes and move to his side? Show the clan she was to be their lady and she'd work beside their laird despite the fact he loathed her?

"M'lady?"

Cam stood watching her with compassionate eyes. "You'll join m'laird on the morrow."

She cast a wistful glance back at Malcolm and those gathered near him. The fiery-haired woman—Fiona—stood on the outskirts of the crowd, her arms crossed before her chest and a scowl clearly etched on her face. Such hateful intensity could be felt across the bailey. Rossalyn narrowed her gaze and observed the woman for a moment before heeding Cam's and her husband's directive and heading toward her new chamber.

They received curious glances from the few who hadn't ventured to greet their laird. She felt Cam nod toward each person they passed, but he didn't stop or attempt to explain her presence. They must think the situation odd, to be sure.

Cam opened the chamber door and she nearly squealed with glee. 'Twas lovely, and after the rough traveling of the past days, a welcome respite. Mairi rushed to the large bed and promptly began jumping upon its surface. Rossalyn laughed and allowed her daughter to have fun after so many days in a wagon. For a moment her troubles seemed to be at bay, off her mind, something to be thought upon on another day. Surely, tomorrow would suit.

The large bed was covered with blankets and pillows. A chest of drawers sat against one wall and rugs and skins covered the stone floor to protect their feet from the cold. A huge fireplace warmed the room to toasty and she appreciated its size, as well as thankfulness that someone had remembered to light the fire when they arrived.

A maid entered, followed by some lads with buckets of water. Ah, a proper bath would make her feel more like herself. She didn't ken if she could talk Mairi into one, but she'd try her hardest. The lass wore the dust of the road about her.

Shivers of awareness trickled over her and she turned toward the door. There stood her husband, leaning lazily against the opening, peering at her with those dark eyes of his.

The lads left to gather more water and the maid scurried to fetch them tea and a slight repast.

And still he stood there watching, his expression unreadable.

"May I help you, m'laird?"

He shook his head and stared as if he wasn't quite sure what to make of her. "I will allow you to settle. Rest and do not even think of coming down for the evening meal. I'll introduce you on the morrow." While his tone was soft, there was warning beneath it and the hard line of his jaw stopped her from arguing.

Still, it bothered her she wouldn't join the clan for the evening meal. "Won't they wonder why we do not join them?"

"They will not question their laird," was all he said before he turned and strode off.

She moved to the doorway, as he left without a glance behind him. She gripped the door to stop herself from following him. He'd made his opinion obvious.

Worry plagued her as she thought upon their fate. If Laird Sutherland remained cold, distant, wouldn't they be better off elsewhere? She'd lived in a keep filled with hatred and violence. While she didn't worry about physical discourse, the indifference her husband had shown her smarted, biting her at the core. Truly she didn't think she could stand to live that way once again.

The maid and lads darted in and out of the chamber in a flurry of activity. Finally, Rossalyn closed the door and leaned upon it.

"Time for a bath, my love."

Mairi continued to jump up and down on the bed. "Nay."

"Mairi, 'twill be quick and then you can eat."

She moved to the table and picked up the linen covering the meal. "There is shortbread."

Her daughter stopped jumping and climbed off the bed. "Shortbread?"

"Bath first." She chuckled when her daughter pulled a face. "Mairi."

"Aye, Mother."

She quickly bathed Mairi, determined her wee lass would smile and laugh instead of feeling worry. As she rinsed Mairi's hair, Rossalyn decided to share what her husband had told her, hoping her daughter would be as excited as she was. "The Laird said we'll celebrate Christmas."

Mairi splashed the water with excitement. "Truly?"

"Aye." She mopped up the water sloshing over the sides of the hip tub. Mayhap she shouldn't have told Mairi, but seeing her so happy was worth it. If Laird Sutherland asked them to leave, she'd beg him to allow them to stay until after the season. Aye, she'd beg. "And dancing and singing." Her daughter's joy was infectious. "And a table full of sweets!"

Mairi's eyes were as wide as saucers. "A whole table?"

She laughed. "Aye, my love. Now dry off and we'll eat."

While Mairi was excited about Christmas, the day had worn her out. Her eyes kept closing as she ate, mostly shortbread, ignoring the roasted carrots and beef stew. Rossalyn couldn't blame her; she was almost too tired to eat herself.

Once they were finished and dressed in sleeping gowns, she guided her daughter toward the bed. While thoughts of the past fortnight tumbled about in her mind, she tidied the chamber. Folding Mairi's dress, she pondered the need for more clothing. Winter was just starting and their present wardrobe would never keep them warm.

"Mother, a story," Mairi called as she climbed into bed with Rossalyn's help.

"Aye, my love." She wiped away the tears wetting her cheeks, then smiled, trying to put on a brave front. Her daughter didn't need to hear her worries. "What would you like me to tell you?"

Mairi thought for a moment, tipped her head to the side and said, "A princess story."

Rossalyn sighed. Her daughter was forever thinking of princes and princesses. As had she, once.

Despite his faults, Daniel had been kind and loving. He took care of them, protected them. So much so, he'd been slain because of his heroism. He was her prince.

Would her new husband be princely?

The hope Laird Sutherland had inspired was gone. She kenned he'd turn them out, return her to her father, even though he'd said he'd introduce her on the morrow. Her—*their*—deceit was too much. 'Twas what she deserved for going along with her father's scheme when she learned about it. But Mairi? Her lass deserved the best, better than she'd done over the years.

She pinched the bridge of her nose, cleared her throat, and began the story of the princess on the beautiful white horse. Within a thrice, Mairi was asleep.

Rossalyn stared at the high, beamed ceiling, wondering, worrying, wasting time being thoroughly annoyed with her new husband. She had no right, aye, she kenned. But she'd hoped they'd be together before the clan. Right before he'd mentioned they would be celebrating Christmas, Malcolm had said he wanted her to be a true lady of the keep. Now, she hadn't a notion if she'd be sent back to Gordon Keep or if Malcolm planned to ignore her, never making her truly his.

And she wasn't certain which would be worse.

Chapter 7

Eyeing the wooden door before him, Malcolm scrubbed his hand over his face and exhaled wearily. He'd tossed and turned the entire night, vexed at himself that Rossalyn plagued his thoughts.

And her daughter. He couldn't get the lass's eyes out of his mind.

Now he stood outside her chamber, trying to determine if he was going to knock on the door or head to the training yard to work with his men. More like work out his frustration in a sparring session with Cam or one of the others. Aye, Cam would do.

Cam had been blunt in his censure of Malcolm's behavior. But damn, he loathed the dishonesty. It festered deep and forgiveness was mayhap too much to expect from him.

Bollocks, he was a fool. His friend's words resonated, what he'd said about Gordon and the keep; about Rossalyn being a gentle woman who deserved better.

Mayhap she did, but could he see past the untruths? Or would he always look at her through a haze of distrust? If only she'd been honest with him. Right when they stood near the wagon, as they stared at each other and couldn't help but reach out and touch. 'Twould have been the perfect time to share what her father did.

She'd remained silent.

Why?

He rapped on the door.

It creaked open and Rossalyn peeked out at him.

All of his rage flew from his mind.

Her black hair hung mussed around her face and her blue eyes glimmered in the early morning light. A rosy blush graced her creamy cheeks.

He opened his mouth to speak and no words came forth. He scraped his fingers over his scalp and gazed at her as she eyed him with uncertainty.

"We need to gather mistletoe," he all but growled and then wondered what had prompted him to talk about mistletoe. Mayhap the lovely, sleepy look of her. Or her dewy skin and those beguiling eyes.

She glanced over her shoulder. "Aye." She shut the door, then quickly opened it again. "I'm sorry, m'laird." A scarlet blush raced up her neck and over her face as she stepped back and allowed him entry.

He entered and saw her daughter was already breaking her fast while propped up with numerous pillows in the large bed. The pillows and bedding nearly engulfed her. His mouth twitched, entertained by the way the wee lass acted as if she were queen.

'Twas a strange set of circumstances. He'd never thought to be responsible for a child before he'd even consummated his marriage. He wanted a wife, bairns of his own, but in time and without the duplicity.

Damn, if only she'd been truthful. If only she'd not lied to him like his former betrothed. How her unfaithfulness stuck in his gut.

He never wanted to experience the pain again. 'Twas why he searched for a chaste wife who'd assure necessities as part of the marriage contract, such as the promise of food stores Rossalyn was supposed to have brought. 'Twas why he pledged not to allow his heart to dictate his actions. Only his clan's needs ruled his desire to wed.

If only Rossalyn didn't look at him that way. Soulful. Sad. He glanced away, then his eyes were drawn to her again.

She reminded him of his mother. A bit of feistiness, but bountiful of heart and love for her child. His beautiful mother had been full of life. She'd deviled his father so; he'd down a dram of whiskey in the morning just to stay ahead of her merriment all day.

When Rossalyn moved toward the bed, all his good humor, borne of his memories, faded as he was once again reminded of her deceit and how she'd made a fool of him.

Rossalyn clutched her hands before her as her gaze flickered between him and her daughter. "I promised Mairi a special treat today."

He nodded. Aye, 'twould have been difficult to keep a lass such as Mairi quiet for the entire trip from Gordon Keep to Sutherland. And now looking at her, eating and grinning from ear to ear, he almost felt sorry for his harsh words. Then she frowned.

What the devil was wrong?

Malcolm stepped forward and settled his hands at his hips. The lass continued to frown at him.

He felt Rossalyn step close. "Mayhap if you didn't scowl so, m'laird."

"I'm not scowling," he protested.

Mairi's bottom lip trembled and he grimaced, then worked to remove any scowl from his face. "No matter. Ensure the lass is dressed warmly."

Ensure the lass is dressed warmly. Did the amadan think she was a liar and a poor excuse of a mother? Rossalyn tossed her hands in the air and grumbled while she gathered Mairi's warmest clothing.

The selection was sparse, so she layered several items. Mayhap Laird Sutherland would provide material for her to make clothing for Mairi before he turned them out.

While she was looking forward to gathering mistletoe—'twas the sign of Christmas, after all—the idea of spending the day with Laird Sutherland unsettled her. The man was in a foul mood and obviously still vexed with her.

Why had he even bothered to ask them to come along if her presence so bothered him? Men were contrary sorts.

"Let's go, pet." She gathered Mairi's hand and they headed toward the main hall.

Curious glances met them as they descended the stairs. She gripped the railing with shaking fingers and her stomach roiled until she feared she'd lose the scone she'd eaten to break her fast. Regardless, she straightened her shoulders and firmed her chin.

A small woman approached them. She had a friendly smile and warm presence about her. "M'laird would like ye to meet him in the bailey, m'lady."

"Thank you—"

The woman waved at her. "Och, me manners. Brae is me name, m'lady."

She smiled and nodded to the woman. "'Tis a pleasure to meet you. My daughter, Mairi."

"A bonnie lass, to be sure." The woman bade them good day and scuttled toward the kitchen.

"Shall we, my love?" she asked with more bravado than she felt.

"Aye." Her daughter bubbled with enthusiasm.

Rossalyn laughed despite her nerves. As they paced toward the bailey, toward Laird Sutherland, she looked about the main hall. 'Twas a large keep, clean and full of clansmen and women. Beautiful tapestries covered the walls, and rugs spread out over the floors. Aye, a lovely keep. She thought upon her former home. Och, how Laird Sutherland must have hated being there. And he'd wed in the main hall, filled with slovenly men, dirt, and foul smelling dogs.

She'd been a fool to think their lives would change. A fool indeed. He'd see he made the wrong choice and they'd be sent out, she kenned it.

They were able to sneak to the bailey without further interruption. Mayhap Laird Sutherland didn't tell the clan who she was or why she was here. 'Twould be odd, but the clan did appear disinterested in her. And what about the woman, Fiona? Her ire was certain to prompt her to tell all.

A wagon filled with furs waited for them and Laird Sutherland sat upon his steed looking like a god in his own right. The sun filtered from behind him, glittering against his dark hair and casting shadows along the expanse of his body, hiding his face and, she presumed, the scowl upon it.

"M'lady?" Cam said as he approached and helped her into the wagon. He lifted Mairi by the waist and tossed her in the air. She squealed with glee.

Laird Sutherland cleared his throat.

Rossalyn glared at him and sat primly in the wagon, doing her best to ignore the beast of a man. 'Twas nearly impossible to do with a man of his size and presence, not to mention how her body betrayed her and thrummed with awareness when he was near.

The wagon driver clucked to the horses and they were fast on their way.

Mairi gabbed excitedly, helping to distract her.

"'Twill do," Malcolm told the wagon driver when they reached a copse of trees. The landscape around the keep was hard and nearly barren. Only a few other groupings of trees littered the horizon.

A strange setting for such a lovely keep.

The more she looked around, the more she understood the Sutherland clan's need for food stores. Dear God Almighty, she prayed her father wouldn't trick her husband.

Panic clenched her stomach. Her father was more than likely to back out of the agreement. As she'd left Gordon

Keep, she'd heard him grousing to his men. Telling them they'd have to work harder to bring in enough stores for both clans. The last thing the Gordon clansmen wanted to do was work harder. Not that the Sutherlands were the only clan benefitting the agreement. 'Twas why her father sought the alliance, to find someone to help protect the borders. It had been increasingly dangerous in the Highlands. Those who kenned Laird Gordon, or had been tricked by him, would no longer help and were often bent on revenge. Revenge which had resulted in the death of some of the guards who traveled the borders.

Rossalyn gripped the side of the wagon until her knuckles turned white. She had to tell him, she had to warn Laird Sutherland. But how? Would he believe her? Would the news confirm his suspicions about her honesty and she'd be on the next conveyance to Gordon Keep?

Once the wagon came to a full stop, Mairi clambered out and started following the driver into the trees. Rossalyn worried her lip as she watched her daughter trot along, so carefree, so happy.

Malcolm dismounted, gathered some tools, and nodded for her to follow. 'Twould be a long day if he chose to remain silent.

Malcolm glimpsed Mairi run after the driver Brun. She chattered and the man listened. He envied her ability to ignore the growing tension between him and his wife.

Sunlight flitted through the canopy of trees, kissing Rossalyn with gold. Something deep within him prodded, until he moved closer. Och, the woman befuddled him. Even now, with her hair tousled loose by the wind, she was incredibly lovely.

"Mother, come and look."

They approached and were privy to the sight of an excited Mairi dragging a bunch of mistletoe behind her. Rossalyn clapped her hands and paced toward her daughter to help her carry the greenery to the wagon.

As she bent to whisper something in her daughter's ear, her cloak parted. Malcolm swallowed. Her creamy breasts, full and luscious, peeked above the neckline of her gown. She tipped her head back and laughed—a throaty peal, filling him with hot lust. His cods nearly burst with need.

Bollocks. He dragged his fingers through his hair and looked away. The damage was done and he felt like a fool as blood rushed to his cock. He grabbed mistletoe and helped Brun with several more bunches, hoping to give his body something to think about besides Rossalyn's breasts.

By midmorning, they had filled the wagon and Mairi was running around the clearing with boundless energy.

Brun brought a basket of food and Rossalyn spread a thick wool tartan over the ground, then unpacked the meal.

As she spoke with her daughter softly, Malcolm listened to her husky voice. 'Twas obvious she adored the lass. And when Mairi threw herself into Rossalyn's arms, he was certain the affection was mutual.

What hell they must have endured at Gordon Keep. He looked away, uneasy with the guilt nudging at his mind and twisting his stomach. Aye, she'd lied . . . but did she have good reason? Would he have done the same in her shoes? Done whatever it cost to ensure his child was safe?

Once again his gaze lit on the wee lass. Precious and innocent. Undeserving of that bastard of a grandsire and the horrid keep. Undeserving of his scorn and the way he'd treated her mother.

Aye, if their positions were reversed, he would lie, even kill to keep his bairn safe.

Mairi looked his way. She grabbed a hunk of cheese and brought it to him. Her steps were hesitant, eyes wide, and a bit of her bravado slipped when she realized he watched her.

"M'laird," she whispered.

Curiosity prompted him to say, "Aye?" as he lowered to his haunches.

She handed him the cheese and then scrambled aside. He looked up at her and grinned. "Thank you, m'lady."

As he hoped, she giggled and tucked her hands behind her back. "I'm not a lady."

He could feel Rossalyn's eyes on them, ever the protective mother. Mayhap she thought him a bastard because of how he'd treated them.

"May I join you?"

Mairi nodded. "'Tis your forest, m'laird."

He threw his head back and laughed. Within a thrice, he'd scooped her into his arms and strode to the makeshift picnic. Mairi giggled the entire time.

He carefully set the child on the tartan and bowed. "M'lady?"

Rossalyn's gaze narrowed and he kenned she was determining if she could trust him not to rush to anger and throw accusations at her.

"Please, Mother," the wee lass begged. "May the Laird sit with us?"

A thin smile tugged at Rossalyn's lips as she gazed at her daughter. Malcolm prayed it would widen and the flash of humor would reach her eyes. When it didn't, he took hold of her hand. She trembled, which pleased him. When she tried to pull away, he held on tighter. Then he rubbed his thumb along the soft flesh of her palm.

"I see you have charmed my daughter, m'laird." Her cool tone didn't deter him.

He lifted his brow. "I was trying to charm her mother," he countered.

She canted her head to the side and cast a suspicious glance toward him. Flashes of distrust flittered about in her gaze and those incredible blue eyes darkened. "I doubt that, m'laird."

"Malcolm," he whispered as he brought her hand to his lips. "Please call me Malcolm."

It seemed like an eternity as he waited for her to speak. His heart pounded against his chest and he hoped he hadn't destroyed her faith in him.

"I'm sorry, Rossalyn," he started after a few moments of heavy silence. "I'm sorry I blamed you for your father's treachery."

The tight lines around her mouth softened. "I knew not what my father planned, but when I realized, I choose to continue deceiving you." Her astute eyes sought his and he saw truth and regret in their brilliant depths. She pulled her hand from his, stood, and gripped her skirt. Tension thrummed around her. "He wanted me to leave without Mairi."

Rage nearly blinded him. If he ever saw the bastard again, he'd kill him. Nay, 'twould be too kind, he'd tear him apart. Limb by limb.

Then guilt flooded his senses anew. "If I had known—"

She held up her hand to stop him. Offered a gentle smile. "Nay, if you had known, you would have refused me."

Bollocks. He rubbed the back of his neck and looked to the horizon. Would he? *Aye.*

"Please allow me to explain." He indicated for her to sit, then sighed when she did. He was being offered a second chance to make his marriage work for him and the clan.

Mairi came and snuggled in her mother's lap. Quicker than he thought possible, her chest rose and fell in slumber. He reached over and brushed her hair from her cheek.

"She's my life." Tears quaked Rossalyn's voice. "Even more so now that her father is dead."

She'd been married and widowed. Left alone to fend for herself and her daughter. Jealously flared before he banked it. How he wished he was the first man she'd loved. Rossalyn was fortunate to have Mairi. "I ken."

She set her hand atop of his. The gesture was reassuring and the warmth of her touch encouraged him.

"Why did you insist on a chaste wife?"

He exhaled. How to tell her when he was so humiliated by the entire experience?

"Malcolm," she said softly.

His gaze met hers and she smiled. And her smile warmed him to the core. "I was to wed another." Damn, 'twas hard to admit to being fooled. "She—she was unfaithful, but still planned to wed me." 'Twas more than humiliating.

He looked down at their joined hands. Hers elegant and soft, his large and callused.

"What happened?"

With a shrug that belied his inner turmoil, he said, "She'd been in love with another. As our wedding approached, he must have decided he didn't want to share." He glanced about the trees. "When he challenged me, I kenned he'd been tupping my betrothed."

She gasped. "Oh, Malcolm."

How he loved the sound of his name on her lips. "Aye. I refused to be challenged. Then I demanded he confess all. And even though she'd been my betrothed and he was one of my guards, they were banished. She tried to convince me he was lying. But I could see it in her eyes when she looked at him." She'd loved the man and at the time Malcolm wasn't willing to settle for a marriage without love, devotion, and honor. Now, his honor and loyalty to his clan dictated the direction of his actions and decision to wed. But his heart 'twas his and his alone.

His wife stroked her daughter's hair as she regarded him. Such compassion radiated from those eyes. "Why was she willing to marry you if she loved someone else?"

He scoffed. "I'm laird." 'Twas the truth of it, and when he realized Trina would be willing to wed him while her heart belonged to another, it astonished him and he closed his heart off to any thoughts of love.

Attraction, aye, he'd allow that. Certainly he was attracted to Rossalyn. A man would have to be dead not to find her desirable.

He tipped up her chin. "'Twas because of her, your deceit stabbed like a knife."

Chapter 8

Her heart ached for him. Och, 'twas hard for a man like Malcolm to admit such a betrayal. Strong men didn't take kindly to being cuckolded. She'd hurt him, she realized. More than hurt him, she'd brought up painful memories he obviously wanted to keep at bay. Shame and guilt ate at Rossalyn.

She'd her reasons, yet now that she'd shared them with Malcolm, the guilt began to lift. "I had to protect my daughter. I had to ensure she would be safe from my father and his men." Tears filled her eyes, blurring the expression of sympathy on Malcolm's face.

"Did they hurt you?" he growled.

Such a fierceness overtook his features and she saw the warrior he could be. Aye, he was magnificent as his jaw clenched, making his face appear to be carved of Highland stone.

She shook her head. "My father made many threats and his men have no scruples. I worried to think of what could happen as Mairi grew." She looked away, finding the truth hard to tolerate.

With her mother gone, 'twould only have been a matter of time before her father married her to someone, just as the clan steward had hinted. And for what it seemed, Laird Sutherland was a decent man and a safe choice for her. Och, if her father had wed her to one of his men she'd would have fled. And then where would they have ended?

He wiped a tear from her cheek with the rough pad of his thumb. "I promise to protect you."

More tears flowed down her face. Mairi moved and jostled herself awake.

She settled herself next to them and peered up with wide eyes.

"Mairi, meet Laird Sutherland," Rossalyn said when she realized they'd never been formally introduced.

Her daughter slowly eyed them both, still sleepy. Then she looked to the ground as she did when her grandsire yelled.

Malcolm chucked her under her chin. "Good day to you, Mairi."

She peeked up at him, a wee bit curious.

He smiled, a brilliant grin with dimples and charm. "I am Laird Sutherland, lass. And your mother's husband." Taking her wee hand in his, he kissed the top as if she were the most fragile thing in the world. "I hope someday you will call me Da."

Rossalyn tried to hold back the tears, but they rushed over her lashes. Mairi didn't remember her father. Daniel had died when she was barely toddling. She'd asked about him and if they were in the privacy of their chamber, Rossalyn would tell her how brave her father was, how they'd met; when he asked for her hand. And how happy they'd been when Mairi was born. Och, 'twas bittersweet.

Rossalyn's heart sang with joy as Mairi's face lit up with a smile.

"Hmmm," Mairi said with a mischievous glint in her eye. "I'm pleased to meet you, m'laird."

Malcolm tipped back his head and laughed. Dear God Almighty, the sound filled the forest with mirth and warmed her heart. He tugged Mairi toward him and she hugged his neck.

Rossalyn swiped at the tears racing down her cheeks. Aye, the man was sweet, to be sure. Her heart nearly melted at his endearing gestures.

They rose to leave—her husband and daughter, Mairi chattering to Malcolm as if she'd known him her entire life. He nodded, laughed, and chatted back.

Rossalyn sighed with relief as she gathered their picnic. Despite her trepidation, she'd made the right choice in bringing Mairi. While she loathed having to lie, she was lucky the laird had a forgiving heart and accepted her daughter.

They were both laughing as they entered the main hall. Rossalyn marveled once again not only at the size of the keep, but its cleanliness as well. Her father loathed wasting energy on something as trivial as cleaning and washing. The Sutherland Keep didn't have food and bones on the floor. The tapestries and furs were free of dirt and, she assumed, mites.

Each clansman worked in some capacity as well. Women carried food to the trestle tables in the main hall, lasses poured ale, and the men brought in peat and wood for the two enormous fireplaces flanking each end of the hall.

They stilled at the threshold. Her nerves began to rattle as clansmen noticed them. Her feet felt as if they were in sludge and she was being dragged to her doom. Would they like her? Or had they heard how she tricked their laird? And was she worthy of such an industrious clan and lovely husband?

"See over there?" Malcom leaned down to Mairi. "'Tis where we will put our tree. And the Yule log will be set in that fireplace for all to enjoy."

"Ohhh!"

Rossalyn envisioned the beauty of the hall during Christmas time. The mistletoe and pine. The merriment and food. Och, how she dreamed of a Christmas feast.

While Father had banned any celebration, little signs of the season usually appeared in parts of the main hall. Her mother's keepsakes, made over the years with care . . . When he tore them down, she'd taken them to her chamber where they'd be safe. Her father had rarely entered her room.

Once her mother died, she'd thought to increase her efforts to make the season one of joy and merriment for Mairi. Something, anything to have hope and not wallow in the despair surrounding them. But her father thwarted her efforts and his men would continue to taunt her about the season and mock her at every opportunity.

"'Twill be lovely," she now said a bit wistfully. Mayhap she'd share some recipes with the cook, a bit of memory in honor of her mother and a way to bring new traditions to the keep. And 'twould be lovely to secure candles on the tree branches and make sure holly berries were sprinkled among the pine.

Malcolm stepped closer, a glint of humor in his gaze and his broad mouth spread into a wide grin. "I promised a merry Christmastime."

His smile was infectious and she found herself grinning. Rossalyn didn't think she'd been so happy in her entire life. Aye, there were moments, but the harsh reality of living in Gordon Keep was a frequent reminder of a joyless life.

Malcolm touched the small of her back and guided her toward the table on the dais. A large chair with ornate carvings was flanked by smaller ones, but clearly no less important.

"Good afternoon," Malcolm called out. The clansmen stilled and turned to face him. Even the serving lasses stopped their toil.

He cast a glance at her before he returned his attention to the interested crowd. More people entered the hall, most likely out of curiosity.

"Clan Sutherland, I present my wife, Lady Rossalyn Gordon, and her daughter, Lady Mairi."

The clan cheered.

"Such a lovely bride, m'laird," a man called.

"Aye," others chorused.

She blushed and cast her gaze to the ground. Men stepped up to slap her husband on the back, bid her welcome, and pat Mairi on the top of her head.

"I ken my journey was to ensure an alliance for food, but when I saw this beautiful woman, I kenned she would be the perfect lady of the keep," Malcolm yelled as he grasped her hand and lifted their arms skyward. "Clan Gordon will provide the goods we need to survive in such an unforgiving terrain. And we will patrol the borders and support Laird Gordon when the need arises."

Cam stepped toward her and bowed. "I pledge my loyalty to our new, and may I say lovely, lady of the keep."

She laughed and Mairi giggled.

"You'll do well to keep your lecherous gaze from my wife," Malcolm warned good-heartedly.

Cam winked. "I'd give him a run for you."

Everything was in place and it pleased him immensely. He had a beautiful woman by his side, a secure agreement with a neighboring clan, and a sweet lass who had captured his heart in less than a day. He'd deal with Gordon, but for now, he wanted his people to feel secure and ready for Christmas.

Many of the clan welcomed Rossalyn and she seemed to respond to them with grace. He'd worried over her ability to care for the clan as a lady would, as his mother had before her death. His time at Gordon Keep didn't bode well. Her father had obviously not allowed her any say in the running of the keep. Mayhap the time before her mother's death had given her the experience she'd need to aid him in the running of his clan.

Yet the fact she'd deceived him continued to fester in the back of his mind. While he kenned her reasons, it still mattered she chose to lie to him.

But he'd made a promise and his word was his soul, his pledge never broken. Their vows were spoken before God. Which meant he'd never forsake his vows.

Seeing her there, before his clan, speaking sweetly to each and every member, eased his mind. The way she tipped her head, to better hear Auld William, made him thankful.

And when her glorious, ebony hair slipped over her shoulder and shifted like a veil of silk, she was incredibly desirable. His gaze traveled over her body, the plump swell of her breasts, the trim waist, the flare of her hips. So womanly, he longed to run his hands over her bare skin and see her writhing with pleasure beneath him.

His cods swelled with such need, he almost swept her into his arms and carried her to the laird's chamber.

She glanced at him, those sapphire eyes holding questions, perhaps concern. He swallowed, knowing his intense gaze was the cause of much of the worry. He inclined his head toward her, trying to show his support.

Malcolm moved to her side as she spoke with the last clansmen.

He pulled her closer, set his hand to her lower back. With each breath she took, his blood surged like a fire through his veins.

Lavender and roses. She must have bathed and used the soap the clanswomen made. In the past he didn't ken why they bothered, but now, as the sweet scent filled him, enticed him, he was more than pleased they did.

"On Christmas Eve, the hall will be filled with even more clansmen and the music will last well until the next morn." He glanced around the hall. "'Twill be a merry time for all."

"I can imagine how beautiful the hall will be." A wistful sigh slipped from her. "Just a fortnight 'til Christmas."

"When I was a lad, neighboring clans would arrive a month early." He shook his head, the memories fresh and vivid before him. "You wouldn't believe the hunting, the games and food. Mounds and mounds of food that nearly buckled the trestle tables."

Until squabbling happened and the clans began to fight as their need for fertile land increased. He thought about the lush landscape surround Gordon Keep. At least they'd have the provisions they needed. He'd secured them, when his father could not. The truth of it, his father had refused to seek Gordon. After meeting the man, Malcolm did not blame his sire. But circumstances had become precarious and as laird he had to take care of his people.

Some of the clansmen broke into song. Rossalyn laughed, a twinkling sound that filled him with something . . . something wonderful and needed.

"To Laird Sutherland and his lady," Auld William yelled. He held up his tumbler of ale in salute.

Several clansmen followed suit, then slowly every person in the great hall cheered. All except Fiona. She hovered toward the rear of the hall, ire clearly apparent in her gaze. He'd have to speak to her, somehow explain the choice he'd made. But 'twould wait. For now, he only wanted to make Rossalyn feel welcome and help her become the true lady of the clan.

And, become his wife in all senses of the word. Just being near her set his blood aflame as she smiled and chatted with the people, so unassuming of her beauty and grace. Didn't she know how desirable she was?

The cook bustled forward. Aye, Aggie had a way about her. The robust woman brooked no nonsense in her kitchen, but made sublime meals.

"M'lady, I'd like a word with ye about the evening meal."

Rossalyn looked surprised. Surely, she'd ensured meals were acceptable at Gordon Keep? But as he thought upon it, mayhap she hadn't, or else their wedding meal would have been palatable.

"I'm certain what you prepare will be more than exceptional," she replied softly. She set her hand on the cook's shoulder and leaned down. "Shall we speak on the morrow? I have some recipes from my mother I'd like to share for Christmas."

Aggie grinned. "Och, m'lady, to be sure! 'Tis glad I am we'll have a lady of the keep for the season."

All progressed smoothly. He was proud of his clan. They talked and raised their tumblers with much jocularity.

'Twas heartening, and Cook's response to Rossalyn spoke volumes—they would accept her.

He kenned it.

"I need to meet with my men." He loathed leaving her side, and for a moment it worried him. Would she distract him from leading his clan? But when she gazed at him, with a twinkle in her gaze and the hint of humor tilting her mouth, he forgot about his concerns.

She nodded. "Mairi should rest." Rossalyn gathered her daughter and strolled from the hall, her womanly hips swaying from side to side to side.

Swallowing, trying to wet his parched mouth, Malcolm rubbed the back of his neck. He knew the risks of their union, knew them keenly. But when a clan needed food the unforgiving terrain wouldn't produce, he had to come up with another solution. Which he had . . .

Marriage to Lady Rossalyn Gordon.

He regarded those still celebrating in the main hall. There he spotted comfort, ease, and clearly, trust. They were pleased with his choice of bride. But did they truly comprehend the consequences? Did they realize he'd exchanged warriors for food? He traded his need of honesty for a woman who'd lied to him from the first moment he'd met her. He'd compromised his morals for a comely face with a soft and welcoming body.

Deep down, he kenned he wouldn't turn her away. For he had a heart and the idea of sending Mairi back to Laird Gordon chilled him to the bone. He clenched his fists at the idea of a beautiful woman like Rossalyn trapped in a keep filled with dishonor and filth.

Instead, he envisioned them together as laird and lady, a tangle of legs and arms as they made passionate love in his large bed.

Blood rushed to his groin and his cock reacted.

He'd need release soon and the only answer he saw was wooing his wife.

Later, the trestle tables were pushed to the sides of the hall. Though 'twas only early afternoon, music began to seep through the great room. Someone ushered Rossalyn back into the main hall, accompanied by wee Mairi, fresh from her nap.

Auld William bowed before Rossalyn and held out his hand.

She smiled and allowed the man to lead her to the center of the hall. People cleared the way and clapped to encourage the couple.

Malcolm scooped up Mairi and eased into the movements of the strathspey dance as he carried her aloft. The lass laughed and clapped her hands. Aye, 'twas a sweet bairn.

After a few moments, he held Mairi toward Cam and strode to claim his wife. She readily accepted his hand and they made their way through the dance with the clan clapping and cheering.

All was content in his world.

Chapter 9

Rossalyn tucked Mairi into bed and sighed. It had been a hectic day filled with activity, noise, and people. She wasn't used to the activity or conversations and her head ached. Och, she shouldn't complain. 'Twas wonderful how the clan welcomed them. With the delay in their introduction and the tension between her and Malcolm, Rossalyn had worried the clan wouldn't be receptive.

She slipped out of the overskirt, then removed her chemise. A maid had left a bowl of water and a linen cloth. Slowly she dipped the cloth in the scented water and washed her face, down her neck, along her shoulder. She moved to dip the cloth once again and startled.

Her husband stood at the threshold.

"M'laird." Rossalyn covered her breasts with her arms. Her heart beat against her chest and her breath caught deep in her throat.

At his hooded gaze, the clench in his jaw, dear God Almighty, her insides melted and her knees nearly buckled. Must he look at her that way? As if he wanted to devour her in one bite?

Please, she wished, *come to me*.

As if she'd spoken the words aloud, Malcolm paced toward her, curled his hand along the back of her neck and delved. Oh, how he delved into her mouth, swift and possessive. His broad mouth commanded hers into compliance, coaxing her lips open.

The heat from his body seeped into hers as her exposed

breasts pushed against his chest. He cupped her bare bottom with large, hot hands.

Such need filled her, a demand to be sated. She'd been alone for so long. Without comfort or the touch of a good man.

She pulled at his shirt, tore at his tartan.

He pushed her hands aside. "Easy, my wife." Malcolm swept her into his arms and carried her across the room. Kicked open the door. Both of them glanced at Mairi, who remained fast asleep.

He brought her to his bed, a huge, intimidating expanse of wood and fur. After he gently laid her upon its surface, he closed the door.

Rossalyn lay naked, but not afraid. And when he came to her side and his gaze moved slowly from her head to her toes, she wanted to clutch at him and pull him atop her.

"M'laird?"

"Aye," he rasped, as if it took all of his strength to do so.

"Are you going to join me?"

Within a thrice his tartan was on the floor and his needy manhood was ready for her. She marveled at the muscular, hard planes of the man.

This was her husband and she couldn't stop smiling.

He lay next to her, stroking her face with the back of his hand. "Are you certain?"

"I've never been more certain." She tangled her fingers through his long hair and pulled his mouth to hers—drank him in as she touched him, explored his body, loving the intake of his breath when she gripped the length of him.

He lapped along her jaw, nuzzled the soft spot behind her ear, all the while whispering so softly she could barely comprehend what he was saying. Yet, she kenned he wanted her.

Malcolm lifted over her, settled between her legs. Aye,

she wanted him, too. She arched toward him, swollen with need, and hissed when his manhood touched her.

"Aye, Rossalyn, aye." He entered her and while she was no maiden, it had been a while. She was tight, but ready.

Slowly he eased in and out, deliberate movements that left her panting. She bucked at each thrust; gripped the sheets, then dug her nails into the hot flesh along his back. Release seemed close, yet she kept it at bay to savor their connection. Aye, she wanted it to last forever.

Malcolm suckled her breasts and she moaned with pleasure.

"It pleases you?" he murmured against her skin as he glanced up at her. His beguiling grin and the hot passion of his gaze had her nodding.

He continued the gentle assault until she was at the tip of a precipice. She hung on, clinging to the pleasure—aye, the pleasure of his touch, the feeling of his manhood within her. She never wanted it to end, even as she longed for the crash of release.

"Look at me," he demanded gruffly.

She complied.

How his eyes flamed with desire as he gazed at her.

He plunged as she rose up to meet him. He shouted his release and she joined him as pleasure shattered over her, rushed through her blood, settled like an explosion within her womb.

They panted together as he collapsed beside her. He pulled her close and she curled next to him as if she'd belonged to him forever and it wasn't the first time they'd joined. Ah, he smelled wonderful, manly, sweaty.

He kissed the top of her head, inhaled; kissed her again.

What the hell had just happened?

He squeezed Rossalyn, partly to feel her against him and

partly to see if she was real and not one of the wee faeries sent to bewitch him. Her soft skin slid against his and he found himself ready to take her again.

Yet Malcolm waited, not wanting to appear as a rutting arse on their first eve together.

Her breath fluttered on his neck, moist, hot. Her hair tickled along his shoulder, reminding him of lavender and roses. 'Twas her breasts that distracted him the most—full, rosy tipped, and pressed against his side as a declaration of her femaleness.

He set his cheek against her tousled hair. Now there was no turning back. The marriage consummated, they were bound by their vows and the joining of their bodies.

Rossalyn yawned, then chuckled. "Are you asleep?"

"Nay." He smoothed his hand along her shoulder.

"I . . . I . . . 'twas wonderful." She glanced up at him, her eyes wide, shining with desire—and something akin to—admiration?

Words caught in his throat, then he was finally able to speak. "Aye." He tipped up her chin and kissed her.

Drawing back, he cupped her chin. "Rossalyn."

"Aye?"

He shook his head and tucked her hair behind her ear. "Go to sleep. We have a busy day on the morrow."

She nodded and snuggled in next to him.

The morning came early. Malcolm snuck a look at Rossalyn, sleeping beside him, and grinned. Her hair, mussed around her face and tangled along her arms, barely covered her breasts. Tempted as he was to ravish her, he rose and began readying for the day. She needed to rest and since their journey, she'd had little opportunity to do so.

His gaze frequently sought her slumbering form. Curled within the linens, Rossalyn slept in his bed as if she had done so every night. The gentle curve of her hips eased into lean legs and delectable toes.

He wanted to suckle them, one by one, until she writhed beneath his attentions.

Damn. His cock hardened. He sent a baleful look in her direction before leaving his chamber to seek out Mairi.

"M'laird," she cried when he opened the door. "Where is Mother?"

He winked and brought his finger to his lips to silence her. "She is sleeping."

Her tiny brow furrowed. "Where?"

Och, out of the mouth of babes. "In my chamber." He'd let Rossalyn explain. "Let us break our fast."

She jumped up and quickly followed him out of the chamber toward the main hall. As they descended the stairs, Cam arrived.

"I see you have a new friend," Cam said as he fell in step next to him. "Such a bonnie lass."

"I'm Mairi."

"Aye, Mairi. 'Tis a grand pleasure to see you." Cam bowed and Mairi clapped her hands in delight. "'Tis said your new family will stay," he said quietly to Malcolm.

Pausing at the hearth, Malcolm settled Mairi in a chair near its warmth, then planted his fists on his hips and regarded the man before him. Cam could be trusted, to be sure.

A few clansmen stilled and hovered by them. There were curious whispers and the blatant stares which told him they weren't certain about his decisions. And now his man, his Sargent-at-Arms, posed questions.

Bollocks, 'twas too much.

"'Tis the truth of it," he finally replied.

Mairi came to his side and took hold of his hand. He glanced down at the wee lass and smiled.

"Do you want to play?" she asked innocently. "When my grandsire was mad, my mother would take me to play."

He tipped his head back and laughed. Och, what a sweet lass. Her words were in turn endearing and troubling, but he was relieved her mother had ensured a safe harbor when Laird Gordon was out of sorts. Such a bastard of a man.

"Aye, let us go and see if we have a pony just your size."

Her eyes widened and a huge smile filled her face. "My mother did promise me a pony a day when I hid—"

Malcolm lifted her onto his shoulders and tried to hold in a chuckle. "When she was hiding you?"

The incorrigible lass nodded.

Cam laughed outright. "You've your hands full with these two."

"Aye." And it didn't bother him in the least.

Even though he barely kenned them, they'd quickly found a way into his family. He looked forward to celebrating Christmas with his new wife and daughter. And in the future, if God allowed, to celebrating with more babes.

Aye, many bairns.

A thread of doubt burrowed in his mind, reminding him to remain watchful. Rossalyn had allowed her father to trick him. A man he'd never trust, but he had to forge the alliance for his clan's sake. What if more treachery loomed? He shook his head to cease such worrisome ponderings. He had to trust her as he trusted his men to guard the keep. If Gordon tried anything, they'd ken.

The future was bright with Rossalyn and Mairi, he must believe it so.

Then Fiona approached and Malcolm groaned. He didn't need further harassment. He lifted Mairi down from his shoulders and pointed her toward the chairs before the hearth.

"So she brought a whelp," Fiona sneered. "You could have had a chaste woman."

Cam scoffed and Fiona sent a glare in his direction.

Malcolm pulled her aside. "You'll never talk to her in

that manner again. Do you ken?" His voice shifted from civil to threatening. Fiona stepped back, but anger narrowed her gaze.

"She used you," she hissed. "You could have had me." She pressed a fist to her chest to emphasize the words spewing from her mouth. "I would have made you happy."

He pinched the bridge of his nose. He hated to feel regret for his friendship with the lass. One that had endured since they were wee, filled with grand memories as he, Cam, and Fiona had played and grown together. Aye, as children not much older than Mairi, they'd said vows the way lads and lasses did when pretending. But damned if Fiona didn't think the vows were true and insisted they were betrothed. No matter how many times he and Cam tried to persuade her otherwise.

"I have chosen the right bride. Vex me no longer."

"We'll see, m'laird. We'll see." Bitterness ringed her tone.

Malcolm turned toward the hearth and the wee lass in the chair before it. 'Twas odd, but he felt a kinship to her despite Fiona's harsh words. And he wanted to protect her from any ugliness. As long as she was beneath his roof, he'd ensure she knew happiness, for he was certain her time at Gordon Keep was anything but.

"Fiona, go to Brae." Cam glared at their childhood friend. "Be certain to tell her how you disgraced the honor of your family with your words and actions."

Fiona gasped as she backed away. "I don't have to listen to you."

"Do it," he warned, "or I will."

She stalked from the room after sending a withering glare at both Cam and Malcolm.

Cam swore beneath his breath. "I'm sorry, m'laird."

He patted his friend on the back. "Not to fret. I should have spoken to her when we first arrived." He worried about her anger. Would she dare confront Rossalyn or be hateful to Mairi?

She was a spirited lass and Malcolm didn't trust her when her ire was up.

"Ensure she realizes I will not allow her to speak to Mairi or Rossalyn in anger."

Cam cocked his brow and settled his hands on his hips. "You ken she's a temperamental woman."

With a laugh, Malcolm acknowledged such truth. Fiona had a frightful anger. When they were young she would retaliate whenever she felt she'd been crossed, with swift fury and a sharp tongue. If she dared to use that viper's tongue on Rossalyn or Mairi, he'd have to decide the consequences. He sighed and dragged his fingers through his hair. Clansmen had seen the confrontation, and so mayhap 'twould be warning enough for no one to speak to his wife as Fiona had. He'd shown he wouldn't tolerate words or actions against Rossalyn and her child.

"Warn her nonetheless. I'll not have my wife hurt by her."

"Aye, your wife, you say." He nudged Malcolm with his elbow. "Your wife."

Malcolm playfully pushed his friend away, ignoring his taunt.

"Mal is smitten," Cam teased.

"*Haud yer wheesh.*" Smitten? Nay. Rossalyn was beautiful and . . . and when they'd joined the evening before—it was glorious. He was a man, after all, and appreciated a comely woman. Was it so horrible he found his wife attractive? Or a disgrace because he yearned to go upstairs and feast upon her again?

Cam now regarded him with wide eyes and a frown on his mouth. "Tell me 'tisn't so."

"What?" he asked as he scooped Mairi up from the chair. She'd been watching them with rapt interest. He hoped she didn't ken what had just transpired with Fiona. He'd have to warn Rossalyn about what had been said.

"You love her."

Malcolm took a step back. "Nay."

Nay, he didn't love her. He wed her for the alliance and that was how it would remain. He wouldn't allow love, which had stabbed him in the back, to make of him the fool, or weaken the foundation on which he led the clan.

"Nay," he repeated.

Cam smirked. "Aye, m'laird."

Mairi pulled on his ear.

"Aye, Lady Mairi?"

"Pony," she said with a pout.

Glad of the distraction, Malcolm chuckled. "To the stables."

Light filtered into the chamber, smarting her eyes. Rossalyn rolled over to pull her daughter close. 'Twas her favorite time of day. When they were warm and safe and still tucked into bed.

She patted the mattress, then quickly sat up and looked around the room. Where was Mairi?

Rossalyn leapt from the bed. Her daughter was nowhere to be seen. She inhaled deeply, trying to steady her rising panic. They were at the Sutherland Keep, not the Gordon Keep. She kenned 'twas safe, Mairi was safe. One quick glance and she sighed. The laird's chamber. She set her hand on her stomach, trying to calm the worry churning it, then hurried to her chamber and dressed so she could search for her lass.

The door opened and her daughter bounded into the room with her usual energy and rosy cheeks.

"I have to show you my pony."

Mairi hadn't stopped talking about a pony since the eve before. Truth be told, she had even spoken of the animal while she slept. Murmuring different names for the pet she so desired, declaring her love for the beast between tiny snores and tossing in the bed.

"Ah, I see you have awakened," Malcolm said as he strode in the room, smiling. 'Twas a good sign and her heart began to patter.

Mairi squealed and dashed to Malcolm, who quickly swooped her into his arms. The grins both their faces wore proved infectious. Rossalyn clutched her chest at the lovely sight before her. Tears of joy tickled at the back of her eyes. Surely her husband would think her mad if she started to weep.

"I trust you slept well," he inquired, eyeing her.

She moved toward him as if she couldn't help herself. His mouth twitched upward and she swore he kenned how his lovely dark eyes enticed her to think thoughts of . . . of his kisses and the feel of his skin beneath her fingers—och, and the way his muscles had flexed against her.

Heat rose over her face; she lowered her gaze and nodded. "Aye."

"Mother, my pony."

Malcolm set Mairi on her feet. "Ah, ah, ah. Not until she has broken her fast."

The lass rolled her eyes and fisted her hands on her hips. They'd only kenned Malcolm for a short time and her daughter was already mimicking his stance. "Hurry." Then her nose scrunched and she asked, "Will I get another pony for Christmas?"

Rossalyn patted her daughter's head. "Enough, my love. I will see your pony, then break my fast."

"I told you, m'laird," she said with a pert tip of her head. "My mother loves ponies too."

Their laughter caught Rossalyn off guard. There had been sadness for too long and the easy shift to humor was unfamiliar. Again she touched her unsettled stomach. 'Twas is if everything was too right with her world. As if she would turn the corner and all of this had been a dream with the nightmare of Gordon Keep, rising before her.

"Is all well, m'lady?"

"Aye." She forced a smile along with the untruth she uttered, and accepted Malcolm's arm.

"My pony is black, Mother. I've named her Sunny."

"'Tis a lovely name."

She clapped her hands. "'Tis what Laird Sutherland said! Didn't you, m'laird?"

Rossalyn glanced at Malcolm and caught the bemused look on his face. Aye, the man was pleasing to look at with his sparkling gaze and his ear held captive by her daughter's chatter. He cradled Mairi as if she were precious. Much like Daniel had done for the short time they spent together as a family.

The image of Daniel kissing Mairi's brow as a babe came to her. He'd scoop her up the minute she'd cried, making coos and promises, then carry on as if he held the best of miracles. Which of course she was. The bittersweet memories assaulted Rossalyn when she should be focused on the happiness of her new marriage.

If only she'd been able to stop the confrontation with her father. If only . . .

"M'laird, m'ladies." The quavering voice brought her from thoughts of guilt and regret. Rossalyn blinked at Auld William, who greeted them as they crossed the bailey. "'Tis a lovely day for the Sutherland Keep, with our laird and lady and the Christmas season quickly approaching."

"That it is, William." Malcolm winked at Rossalyn and heat flooded her despite the chill in the air.

"I have a pony," Mairi announced.

"'Tis grand," Auld William said. "I'll be by to visit her in a thrice."

Mairi nodded and chattered the entire way to the barn, equally enthralled with the pony *and* Auld William's pending visit.

"There she is." Mairi wiggled out of Malcolm's arms and raced to her new friend.

"'Tis a large pony," Rossalyn said with alarm. Her daughter barely reached the animal's belly. She gripped Malcolm's arm. "Is it safe?"

He caught her hand and twined his fingers with hers. His warm palm chased heat throughout her. Dear God Almighty, her body was quick to react. She was a wanton woman, to be sure.

He nodded. "The pony is safe, I assure you."

"I never meant to imply otherwise. Mairi is still so wee."

A gentle smile tipped up one side of his mouth. "I ken you are a concerned mother, Rossalyn—"

Caustic, intruding words interrupted him. "Well, well, well."

'Twas that woman. The beautiful lass who rode with abandon and threw herself into Malcolm's arms.

"'Tis a cozy family."

Malcolm's muscles clenched beneath her touch. Rossalyn spied the rapid pulse along his jaw, a sign of vexation, to be sure.

"*Fiona.*"

"Not to worry, m'laird," she sneered with a wink. "I'm certain you won't be needing me when you have her."

Rossalyn opened her mouth to tell the woman she was a rude lass.

"Mother," Mairi called.

Rossalyn sent an apologetic glance toward Malcolm and crossed to her daughter's side.

"Isn't she beautiful?"

"Aye, she is." Rossalyn tried but couldn't prevent a scowl from forming as she glanced at Malcolm and Fiona.

Her daughter gripped her hand and pulled. "*Look*, Mother."

Rossalyn made herself refocus on her child. Och, she was acting like a shrew. Malcolm had kenned Fiona since they were bairns. She'd no right to interfere. And, from the thunderous frown her husband wore, no reason to worry as anger darkened his face.

Even so, as she petted the pony and made enough appreciative sounds to please her daughter, her gaze never left her husband and his childhood friend.

Fiona tossed her hair over her shoulder and glanced back at Rossalyn. How did the woman get it so shiny and smooth? Not that she'd ever ask, but 'twas vexing, nonetheless.

"Look at her run." Sunny had turned from her new owner and trotted around the small area Malcolm had fenced in for her.

Rossalyn chuckled. "She's lovely."

Mairi's grin couldn't get any bigger. Her daughter was smitten and Rossalyn feared she'd want to sleep with the beastie as well.

She turned toward the sound of tinkling laughter. Ire raced through her as Fiona had snuggled close to Malcolm, touching his arm.

Why didn't her husband step away or tell the woman to stop? As she scrutinized them, he looked down his nose at the wench, but he didn't move or push her hand from his forearm. If only she could hear what he was saying.

Fiona cast her a smirk that said, "Aye, I'm touching your husband."

Rossalyn hiked up her skirt and strode to Malcolm's side. Uncertainty and a touch of sadness flitted in Fiona's eyes for a moment and then she quickly tipped up her chin in a haughty action.

"M'laird, the pony is a lovely present for Mairi."

He nodded as relief visibly brightened his expression, and he moved toward her. "They are well suited."

"Please join us and then I can speak with Cook. 'Tis the duty of the lady of the keep, after all." Rossalyn would not resist that small taunt.

If possible, Fiona's glare would have flung daggers.

"Mairi," Malcolm called. "We'll visit your pony later."

"M'laird, I'll stay with the lass," Auld William called as he slowly approached. "She's safe with me." He made a point to look at Rossalyn after he spoke. As if he were stating *she's one of us now.*

"Thank you," Rossalyn said, accepting Malcolm's arm. They walked back toward the keep's entrance.

Frustrated silence filled the air. Och, would the man say something? 'Twas as if he'd lost his tongue.

"Don't let her anger you," he warned. "'Tis what she wants."

Finally. "Aye, well. I'm the one you married, aren't I?"

He tipped his head back and laughed then quickly kissed her brow. "And glad I am, at that."

Dear God Almighty, her heart filled with such happiness. She reached to grip his broad shoulders, stretched to her toes, and kissed his mouth. After a moment of surprise, he pulled her to him, swooshing the air from her lungs, circling her waist with his hands.

As they kissed, the sounds of the clan disappeared and 'twas as if they were the only people in the Highlands. If possible, her heart surged even more full. Of happiness—of love.

She pulled away from him. Narrowed her gaze as she inspected his face. She'd kenned this man for such a short time. Could she love him? He made her feel safe, wanted. And when he wasn't there, her thoughts were only of him. Aye, she thought, she loved him.

Rossalyn cupped his cheek with her hand and slowly brushed her thumb over the stubble along his strong jaw. The endearment burst forth.

"I love you."

Chapter 10

Her eyes widened in surprise even as the words came out of her mouth. God, she was lovely. Her eyes, bright and intelligent, seemed to ken all. They sparkled when she smiled, bringing light to the depths of blue.

'Twas as if Rossalyn saw his soul and still wanted to learn more.

And she'd just said she loved him.

Her lips parted, a direct invitation. Malcolm wouldn't leave her wanting. Nay, he thought as he descended, as their lips met—'twas as if he were home. For a moment he almost pulled away, for he'd been made a fool before, his heart battered.

But when her lips parted and she tangled her fingers through his hair, he pushed his thoughts aside.

He smoothed his hands over her shoulders, his large palms itching to reach for her and cup her breast. His cods ached for her.

Malcolm eased from her and stared at her face. Her breath came in spurts and her hooded gaze nearly had him ravishing her in the middle of the bailey. A smile curled her kiss-swollen lips, and he felt it. Felt it deep within him.

Love.

Malcolm leaned his forehead against hers. Her confession confused him. Nay, it worried him.

He'd pledged not to love.

But as he looked into the eyes that so enthralled him, mayhap 'twas time to let go of the past. She grinned. He loved how her lids tipped up at the corners and how flecks of silver swirled in the sapphire depths. *Bollocks*, now he was waxing poetic about a lass's eyes.

"Go," he rasped, as he tapped her nose. "'Tis almost time to ready the tree for the main hall."

At the way she clapped her hands and squealed, Malcolm laughed. "I'll send Mairi in to rest soon."

Rossalyn strode across the bailey and greeted clansmen as she entered the keep. He gazed at her, proud she was his, proud she'd lead beside him.

"M'laird, would you care to go riding with me?"

He sighed at the appearance of Fiona. "Nay," Malcolm said as he confronted his childhood friend.

She gripped his arm. "Has she turned your head against your clan?"

Malcolm rubbed at his temple. Frustration led him to retort, "Nay. My people are my first concern."

He had wed Rossalyn out of worry for his clan, his people. To ensure they'd a leader whose woman cared for his family as he did.

She slapped her hands on her hips. "Aye, she has. And how do you ken she will be true to you or the clan?"

Anger surged through him. Fiona knew his anguish after his betrothed had made a cuckold of him. How he'd been deemed a fool right before his clan. When he'd announced his intent to wed, Fiona had said nary a word. She hadn't brayed then, as now. Had she kenned Trina loved another, and the wedding would never happen? Did she expect the betrothal to be broken? Would Fiona have dared keep such a secret from him?

He frowned as she moved a step toward him. "Do you think about you and me? When we were a lad and lass, swimming in the creek and then riding across the land?"

"We were bairns. And now friends, clansmen, nothing more."

She came closer. "I would be good to you, Mal." Fiona trailed her finger along his arm.

He caught her hand and removed it from his arm. "I will remain true to my vows. Rossalyn is my wife, Fiona, not you."

Fiona glared at him with a jerk of her chin. "And how do you ken she'll stay true to you? You've made that mistake before." She spun to leave and halted when she saw Cam standing with his arms crossed before his chest.

"What are you doing, Fiona?" he growled.

"'Tis none of your concern." She stomped off.

Malcolm would have to do something about her, though he wasn't certain what might be best. His gaze lit on Mairi, chattering to Auld William. The man chuckled as Mairi giggled and pointed to her pony.

A stable boy led the beastie over to her. And the wee lass jumped up and down.

"Fiona will come around," Cam said. "The lass needs time to adjust to the change."

"Mayhap." But he'd serious doubts. Fiona's tenacity warned she'd not stop until she gained a boon. How could she still believe they were to be man and wife?

"Keep an eye on her. If she vexes my lady, tell me."

Cam gave a mock salute. "Will do, m'laird."

Malcolm sighed, then crossed to where Mairi entertained Auld William and some of the clansmen.

"Shall we ready the tree?"

Her eyes widened. "Aye." She held out her hand.

Malcolm stared for a moment, swallowed, then grasped her wee fingers.

She babbled the entire way to the main hall.

"M'laird, are you ready to set the tree?" Brae called.

"I get to help," Mairi boasted.

Malcolm grinned when the woman winked. "Lucky lass."

"Brae, can you send a lass to fetch my wife?"

The woman cackled. "Fetch her, you say?"

"No need, Brae. I'm here." Rossalyn moved forward. "I'm so excited to help, I couldn't concentrate on the menu." Her eyes glittered and a full grin curved her luscious mouth.

One glance at her hopeful face and he kenned. Everything about her cast aside what Fiona had said. He wasn't certain he trusted her fully, but he'd give her a chance.

"Mother, we're going to decorate the tree!"

"Aye, my love." As she spoke to Mairi her gaze never left Malcolm's face.

It warmed him to the core and he yelled, "Come, clansmen. Help us place the tree."

Cam led six other men who hefted a giant evergreen into the main hall.

People clapped and cheered.

'Twas as if they were back in time and his father led the beginning of the Yule season.

After the men had secured the tree, Malcolm lifted Mairi onto his shoulders and handed her a candle. "Set it on one of the branches."

Rossalyn came close, so close he inhaled the feminine essence of her. She reached up, and as their bodies brushed, heat filled him. Her blue eyes sought his and red stained her cheeks.

She secured the candle base on the limb as Mairi giggled.

The happiness surrounding him, he would credit to the lovely woman beside him and her enchanting daughter. Och, if only his parents had lived to meet her. The thought sobered him for a moment before Mairi was patting his head for another candle.

One of his clansmen shouted, "M'laird, 'tis riders approaching. Wearing Gordon plaid, they are."

Rossalyn gasped.

He eased Mairi off his shoulders, remaining calm when he wanted to reach for his sword and rush to the bailey with it raised high. "Remain inside the keep, no matter what happens."

"Aye, Malcolm."

He nodded and strode from the main hall to see what new threat lay outside the gates.

Sweat coated Rossalyn's palms and her heart ratcheted against her chest. 'Twas Father with the riders, she felt certain. Did he discover she'd escaped with Mairi?

Aye, he must have.

She urged Mairi to the back of the main hall, away from those still gathered around the tree and adding candles.

Such a joyous occasion, ruined by her fear of her father.

"'Tis men from your clan?" a voice said behind her.

Rossalyn spun around and stared at Fiona. "Aye."

Fiona gripped her arm and pulled her farther away from the clansmen. "Mayhap you should leave through the back. Won't he be vexed at Malcolm if he discovers her?" She glanced at Mairi. "I've heard he is a violent man."

Had Malcolm told Fiona of her treachery? Rossalyn moved in front of her daughter. She'd hate for Malcolm to experience her father's wrath. Panic filled her. What if he ended up like Daniel? Images of her dear Daniel, bloodied and dead, flashed before her. She must keep Malcolm safe, no matter the circumstances. "Where would we go?"

"I ken just the place," Fiona whispered.

She had to save Malcolm. Save the man she loved. "Take us there. Now."

She gathered up her skirt and gripped Mairi's hand. Fiona led them through the kitchens and to the back of the keep. As they rushed along, Fiona snatched tartans which were hanging on a peg. They entered the back of the bailey and raced to the stone perimeter.

"'Tis a door right there." Fiona pointed to the iron gate in the stone palisade. "When you are outside the wall, run to the woods, they'll never find you there."

Unease prompted Rossalyn to say, "What about Malcolm?"

Smiling, Fiona shoved them toward the gate. "I'll let him ken where you went. Once the men are gone, he'll come for you."

"Please have him tell my father's men I'm heading back to Gordon lands. Tell them . . . tell them Malcolm rejected me because of Mairi." They'd have to determine a plan to deal with her father in the future, but at this moment, she must get Mairi to safety.

The woman nodded. "Grand idea, m'lady."

Rossalyn felt wretched over the evil thoughts she'd had about this woman, now that she was helping them and Malcolm. She gripped Fiona's hands. "Thank you."

Fiona shook her head. "I'm doing my duty to my clan. We can't have the laird of the keep injured, can we?"

Feeling a bit of relief, Rossalyn gathered Mairi and they scurried to the gate. It creaked open, but no one seemed to notice. She heard shouting and kenned her father was with the men. They had to get away—to keep all of them safe.

When she wasn't found, Fiona would provide the easy explanation of how Rossalyn had left to return home. Her father would certainly not balk at that.

"Run, Mairi," she prompted her daughter.

They raced to the copse of trees.

From their vantage point, Rossalyn saw her father and his men yelling at the gate. She couldn't make out their words, but fury marked their gestures.

Please, she prayed. *Do not let Malcolm be harmed.*

Chapter 11

"Gordon."

The man barged forward, still astride his steed. The rest of the men gathered behind him. "Where's me daughter?"

Malcolm braced his arms across his chest and stared down his nose at the odious man. "Do you mean my wife?"

Gordon moved to dismount his horse. Malcolm's men unsheathed their swords and took a step forward.

"What do you want us to do, Malcolm?" Cam moved to his side.

"Stand down. For now."

Taking in the men before him, he decided he had two options. Let his clansmen loose, or invite the bastard in to see his daughter was safe and sound.

"Don't threaten me, Sutherland. She took something that was mine."

Now they were getting to the meat of it. He met the man's gaze straight on. "Ahh, do you mean *her* daughter Mairi?"

A flicker of surprise flashed in the auld man's eyes. "Aye, she was to stay with me. You've taken my daughter away from me and the lass is the only kin I have of her."

His horse sidestepped. Gordon swore and his men encroached further.

"All right then. I'll show you to your daughter." Malcolm nodded to his clansmen.

All of the men started to dismount. "Nay," he growled in a low voice. "Only Gordon."

Rossalyn's father held his gaze for a moment, then

waved off his men. "Stay alert. If Sutherland's men take one step closer, you will engage."

Malcolm scoffed aloud at that.

"Are you certain you don't want us to run them through?" Cam asked with a bloodthirsty grin.

Malcolm turned toward Cam. "I will have him see Rossalyn and Mairi and then force him to leave."

"And if he doesn't?" Cam asked as he rubbed his chin.

His man was itching for a fight. "He will meet his maker." And Malcolm would be more than happy to be the one who dispatched Gordon to hell. The man had made Rossalyn's and Mairi's life pure misery. A man needed to be punished for such actions.

He nodded toward Gordon. "This way."

They strode to the main hall. "Wait here while I get them."

Malcolm searched the chamber for his wife and Mairi. They weren't there. He looked in the kitchens and main hall. All to no avail.

"Where's me daughter?" Rossalyn's father demanded when Malcolm returned to him.

He cocked a brow at the man, not certain he wanted to share he didn't ken where his wife was. "Tell me, Gordon. You were quick to wed her off, why do you want her now?"

"Och, lad." The laird removed his tam and twisted it in his hands. "'Twas wrong of me to force her to wed."

An icy chill ran down Malcolm's spine. He didn't believe the man, to be sure, but there was something else he couldn't name that his instincts warned him about. "Do you mean to go back on our deal?" If the bastard was going to break the contract, there would certainly be hell to pay.

Gordon grimaced, then held up his hands. "Now, Sutherland. If my daughter doesn't want to be married to ye, then aye, the deal will not take place." He shrugged his shoulders. "But if she does want to remain, then we'll continue forward."

Malcolm didn't believe him. In fact, he thought the man was purposely trying to retain Sutherland warriors and keep his daughter. Which he would not allow. Nor would he let the man take her or Mairi.

Gordon rested his hand on the hilt of his sword. "Where is she, Sutherland?"

He merely cocked his brow at the sword. His men were nearby in case they were needed, but Malcolm had no doubt he'd best the old man in a sword fight. More important was the location of his wife. Where was she?

He spotted Brae, coming from the kitchens. "Brae, have you seen m'lady?"

Surprise lit the woman's features, then worry etched across her brow. "Och, she was here a moment ago, m'laird."

Brae started toward the main hall, searching, as Malcolm followed. Where was his wife? Had Gordon distracted him while one of his men took her?

Nay, he thought as he dragged fingers through his hair, his clan would have stopped such a deed.

"Are you well, Mal?"

He turned and glared at Fiona. He crossed his arms before his chest and asked, "Have you seen my wife?" In his gut he kenned the answer. Fiona was bound to cause trouble. 'Twas his fault he didn't speak more directly to her; threaten consequences to her actions, regardless of what she thought.

She blanched and looked to the ground.

He came within a step of her. "What aren't you telling me?" He growled so loudly, clansmen gathered around, hovering close. He wanted to yell for them to go, search for his wife.

"I hate to be the one to tell you—"

He gripped her arms. He would get the truth from the woman. "I doubt that."

She lifted her chin, but her gaze shifted and he kenned the look. 'Twas guilt.

"Do you wish to ken where she is or not?"

"What have you done?" He peered right into her eyes. She held his gaze for a moment, then glanced away. "Tell me now, woman."

She tried to shrug out of his grip. "I saw her leave."

Malcolm jerked back. "*Leave*?"

Clansmen gasped as Gordon sputtered.

"Cease," Malcolm ordered as he dragged her into the main hall. "Are you certain, Fiona?"

Fiona's eyes glittered with animosity. She jerked away from his hold. "Aye, she said she was headed back to Gordon territory."

"What?" Dear God, she'd taken wee Mairi and left him.

"She grabbed her daughter and snuck out the back gate." Fiona's jaw flexed and she straightened her shoulders. "I told you, Mal."

Something in her tone irked him, set his instincts on alert.

At his lifted brow, she turned contrite. "I'll gather the women to help look for them."

"Stay here," Malcolm growled, then shouted, "Brae!" The woman scurried from the kitchens. "Send one of the men to Cam and have him start a search party. M'lady has fled to the wood."

Gordon pushed between them. "Me daughter is out there on her own?"

Malcolm tried not to throttle the man where he stood. "You had no concern for your daughter when you forced her to wed me."

The man grimaced and scrubbed his hand over his face. "Och, 'twas the clan I was thinking of."

Cam and some of his strongest men came forward. "We're ready, m'laird. I left half guarding Gordon's men."

Gordon shifted to accompany them.

"Nay, remain where you stand. Ian, watch over him and do not let any of his men leave." To Brae he ordered, "Have the women gather blankets and hot food."

Ignoring Rossalyn's father as he cursed him for being a 'bastard,' Malcolm and Cam exited the keep and paced to the rear gate, clansmen and women with hurriedly-collected supplies following behind.

Then snow began to fall.

Rossalyn and wee Mairi were in the forest, in the cold.

Shoving his fears aside, Malcolm pushed forward. If he wallowed in those fears, 'twould do nothing to save his family.

"We must find them!" he shouted to his clansmen.

Malcolm didn't ken when Rossalyn had gone from a wife of necessity to someone he cared about, but it seemed the change had happened in a thrice. Naught he could do about his heart becoming hers.

Rossalyn dragged Mairi through the snow-covered thicket and toward the copse of trees where they'd gathered mistletoe. They had to hide from her father. For she'd rather die in the woods than go back to Gordon territory.

Not that she'd put her daughter at risk. Poor dear had a rough time of it with her wee legs. They must find a cave or some fallen trees in which to hide.

"Mother," Mairi said. "I'm hungry."

In their haste to leave they had the tartans, but she'd not grabbed more than a blanket she'd seen on a chair near the door. No food or warmer clothing.

What a fool she'd been. In fact, they'd all been fools to think her father would keep his word. Now she and Mairi were hiding in the woods and who kenned when Malcolm would realize where they were?

Please, she prayed, *find us soon.*

She couldn't help but feel the coward. She glanced at Mairi, trembling in the cold. 'Twas her daughter she thought of when she fled—and Malcolm.

Dear God Almighty, if something happened to either of them, she'd never forgive herself.

"Come, Mairi. We must hurry." Why hadn't she asked Fiona to hide Mairi somewhere in the keep? She'd stay warm and Rossalyn would lead her father into thinking she was returning to Gordon territory.

Much to her daughter's credit, she didn't complain. Truly another pony wouldn't be out of the question.

She gripped Mairi's hand tightly as they trudged up a hillock. There had to be a place to hide. Then Rossalyn spied several fallen trees through the snow. A perfect place for concealment.

She pointed to the trees. "Over there, my love."

They reached the trees and Rossalyn wrapped the blanket around Mairi, then pulled her daughter onto her lap. Hopefully her body would keep her wee one warm enough. After they hunkered down, Rossalyn tucked tartans around them to ward off the cold and falling snow.

"Come close, Mairi. I will keep you warm." *Please*, she prayed.

She hummed to her daughter and rubbed her arms to help keep her warm.

If Malcolm came to her, she vowed to fight her father. He'd ruled her life with fear since her mother died and more so after Daniel's death. How much would she continue to sacrifice to the vile man?

For her fear of him already cost her one husband.

Chapter 12

"Search behind every rock or tree," Malcolm bellowed to the men. His blood roared and his heart pounded nearly as fierce. He had to find them.

"M'laird, there are tracks heading toward the north," Cam called.

Thank God for the fresh snow. 'Twould make tracking his wife and Mairi easier. When he thought of them in the cold, rage rushed through his veins. *I swear I'll kill Gordon and send Fiona away.*

Both had caused his wife too much pain.

Malcolm pushed up the hill, keeping a keen eye on the footfalls before him. "Span out, we need to cover enough land."

Several women followed with warm clothing and a bag of hot food. When they found his wife and Mairi, they'd certainly be cold.

Why had Fiona let her leave, and flee into the forest without as much as a horse or provisions? Och, he knew the reason. Her jealousy had blinded her against good sense as well as her loyalty to her laird and his lady.

He could throttle both women; Fiona for allowing Rossalyn to leave and Rossalyn, for tearing out his heart. If anything happened to her, he'd . . . He'd—

He loved her.

Had she'd chosen to go back to Gordon Keep?

Didn't she declare her love? Why would she leave him, a man she professed to love, for a keep she equated to hell?

He pushed forward, eager to get to his wife and their daughter.

He had to discover why Rossalyn wanted to leave when she'd said she loved him, forcing him to search for her in the midst of a snowstorm and frigid temperatures.

"M'laird, we've found them."

Malcolm ran to where his men stood. He knelt onto the snow and with shaking hands lifted his wife, as one of the women gathered Mairi into her arms, wrapping her in a cloak.

"Rossalyn?" He shook her and hugged her close. "Rossalyn?"

She wriggled in his tight grasp. "Mairi? Where is she?"

He swept flakes of snow from her eyelashes. "She is well, m'lady," he whispered close to her cheek and inhaled her lovely scent. His heart battered against his chest.

Rossalyn cupped his face with icy hands. "Malcolm, my father—did he hurt you?" In the moonlight, her steady gaze searched his face.

He grinned at the thought of a man as auld as Gordon causing him harm. "Nay, my love. He awaits us at the keep."

Panic widened her eyes. "You must make him leave." She gripped his jacket. "He will kill you."

Malcolm furrowed his brow. "M'lady, you're distraught." Did she really think her father would kill him?

He lifted her into his arms, his men flanking them as they descended the hillock. "Secure Gordon's men. Then meet me in my chambers." He had to get his wife and Mairi warm.

Malcolm carried her into the bailey and then the keep. Cam followed with Mairi clasped close.

Gordon bellowed after them as Malcolm took the stairs two at a time. "Let me see me daughter."

Malcolm ignored the man and continued his hurried stride.

"Get hot water," he demanded of the serving lasses. "Gather blankets and stoke the fire."

His wife shook like a leaf in his arms. He felt it to his core. One glance at Mairi, still in Cam's hold, and his heart sank. So pale, he kenned on the morrow she could fall ill.

"Wrap the bairn in blankets." He glanced about. "Add more wood to the fire in m'lady's chamber."

Rossalyn touched his arm. "All will be well." She snuggled closer to him, the chill of her skin seeping into his. He gazed at her, this beautiful woman, who now curled her hands into his jacket as if clinging for dear life. He carried her to the laird's chamber.

Why did she leave? He had to ken.

He brought her to their bed, where they'd made love.

A lass came to the door. "M'laird, the lady Mairi is awake and asking for porridge."

He grinned despite the situation. "Aye, and make sure she has warm milk as well." With a quick nod around the room, he added, "Leave us."

The women and men who'd help find his wife and child exited the Laird's chamber within a thrice.

Rossalyn sighed and reached for him when he placed her upon their bed. "Please, don't let go."

His stomach quivered with something unfamiliar, something akin to stark need for her. She eyed him smilingly, and his heart leapt. Surely, she didn't want to leave him.

Determined to find out why she had run, Malcolm knelt by her side and gathered her hands within his.

"Why did you flee?" He smoothed his thumb along the soft skin of her hand. "You nearly frightened me to an early grave."

"Surely you wouldn't have missed us."

Malcolm cocked a brow. "Do you doubt my words?"

She shifted so that she leaned toward him. "Nay, my

husband." Rossalyn trailed her finger along his jaw, over his bottom lip. He kissed the slender digit.

"Why?"

Her brow furrowed. "Where is my father?"

"I will ensure he'll never darken our door again."

"How will you manage such a feat?"

"I have a plan. 'Twould be within Gordon's best interest to obey."

Pounding rattled the door. "Let me see me daughter."

Every time the man had asked to see Rossalyn, he failed to mention Mairi. 'Twas obvious the bastard cared naught for the wee lass. And when they'd wed, Malcolm would have bet the keep Gordon held no love for his daughter.

"Leave us be, Gordon," he shouted.

The man continued to pound.

She glanced toward the door. "He will never leave us be."

"I've my ways, wife." He tipped up her chin, vowing no need to worry her with the details. "Why did you leave me?"

"Fiona didn't tell you?" Her frown deepened. "I asked her to."

Anger unfurled in the pit of his stomach. Fiona had lied to him. In the past, he'd have trusted her and Cam with his life. Now, he could only say that about one of his childhood friends. "She said you left to return to Gordon lands."

Rossalyn lifted from the bed and pulled him toward the window overlooking the keep. He placed his arm around her shoulders and kissed the top of her head.

"I left, dear Malcolm, because I didn't want my father to hurt you . . . like he did Daniel."

She shivered and he held her tighter. He'd deal with Fiona later.

"Your first husband?" Mairi's father and Rossalyn's first love. He banked the rising jealousy. Without Rossalyn's first husband, there wouldn't be Mairi, and the world had need of such a beautiful lass. "Tell me about him."

Though her father still pounded on the door, Rossalyn paid no heed, as if she had great practice doing so in the past. 'Twas driving Malcolm to distraction, but his wife needed no more drama for the evening.

She shrugged. "He was a fine man, kind and devoted to us. But he—he had a penchant for vexing Father and 'twas the final argument which led to his death by my father's hand."

"Your father killed your husband?" The man was the very devil himself. *When I get my hands on the bastard, I'll surely murder him.* "If I'd kenned, I promise I would have gotten revenge." He *would* exact revenge for all of the pain Gordon caused Rossalyn and Mairi.

She spun to face him. "Nay! The man will stop at nothing to hurt those I love."

He cupped her cheek in his palm. "Do not worry. I will never allow him to hurt you or Mairi ever again."

Tears glittered in her eyes and she leaned against his hand. So intimate and tender, emotion welled within him and he swore his heart expanded.

"Rossalyn, I have to tell you—"

The door burst open. Gordon landed on the floor.

Malcolm turned and advanced on the man. Rage billowed around him, all the pain the bastard had caused surging forth. He heaved Gordon to his toes and slammed him into the wall. "How dare you enter my chamber without permission," he growled in the laird's face.

All the color leeched from Gordon's skin. "Let me go."

Malcolm crushed the man against the stone wall.

"Nay." Rossalyn pulled at his arm. "He's not worth your anger."

"Listen to your wife, Sutherland. No good will come of killing me."

He sneered at Gordon. "Aye, plenty of good. The world would be rid of you."

"Malcolm," Rossalyn begged. "Don't sully your hands with him. 'Tisn't worth it."

After a glance at his wife and the mix of uncertainty and fear on her face, he let go and Gordon crumpled onto the floor. Then staggered to his feet and lumbered toward Malcolm.

Malcolm crossed his arms before his chest. "Stand your ground, auld man."

"Father, you have no power here." Rossalyn moved closer to Malcolm. "You will leave and Mairi and I will remain at Sutherland Keep."

Her father glared. "I'll no listen to a lass. 'Tis business between men and I'll do as I please."

"Tell me, Gordon. Why did you come to Sutherland Keep?" Malcolm clenched his fist tight, lest Gordon would feel their weight upon his jaw.

"I missed me daughter." He offered Rossalyn a smirk. "She and the whelp are all I have."

Malcolm took a step forward. The flickering light of the fireplaces played over the auld man's face. He looked like the devil he was. And 'twas obvious he was lying. "The real reason?"

Gordon's beady eyes skittered between Rossalyn and Malcolm. "'Tis the truth of it. After she left, I had nightmares of me wife vexing me. And I ken it was because I forced our daughter to wed."

Rossalyn tossed up her hands. "Mother was as gentle as can be."

Malcolm lifted his brow and grinned at his wife. While he appreciated the sweet, tender woman he'd married, he liked to see her spirit, especially since she used her ire against the man who'd caused her so much turmoil.

"Why did you come?" she pressed. "You hold no love for me or my daughter."

"Och, you took the lass." Gordon's face darkened and stormy fury gathered in his eyes as tension drew tight and hot in the chamber. "She was to stay with me." He pounded his chest. "Me."

Rossalyn gave a humorless laugh. "Never." She stared her father down. "You care not for her."

"Aye, the lass matters not to me," he said with a sneer, then he shrugged. "But to you—to you she matters."

Rossalyn gasped. Malcolm reached for her and hoisted her back just as she poised to launch herself toward Gordon. She flailed her arms, trying to grab at her father. "You bastard. You would dare leverage my daughter against me?"

"Easy, my wife. He can't hurt you now." Malcolm held Rossalyn against him. He kissed her brow. "I will protect all in my household."

"Even the whelp of her bastard husband? She isna' yers, Laird Sutherland."

"It matters not who her father is. She is my wife's daughter and now she is mine."

Rossalyn turned to look up at him. "Truly?" Her expressive eyes glittered with love as she waited for him to answer.

Och, his wife was beautiful.

"Aye."

"Enough of yer blathering!" Gordon roared. "The lass was to stay with me. If ye backed out of the deal, then I'd be able to force me daughter's hand."

She lurched toward him in fury. Malcolm circled his arm around her waist to restrain her. Without taking his eyes from Gordon, he said, "Nay, wife. Go and warm yourself by the fire while your father and I have a discussion."

He waited until she nodded, then released her. Rossalyn crossed to the fireplace, but stopped and eyed both of them.

Worry etched her brow. Finally, she sat but her gaze stayed pinned on him.

"You will leave Sutherland territory," he directed at Gordon. "You will never show your face on my lands again."

Gordon sputtered. "But the contract—"

"Aye, the contract."

They needed each other. 'Twas the rub of the situation. Sutherland needed the food stores. Mayhap more than Gordon needed men guarding the borders. His rabble of clansmen could make do if they chose to get off their arses and lift a sword in defense of their own.

"I'm an honorable man. I will not forsake the contract." He rubbed his hand along the hilt of the sword hanging about his waist. "As long as *you* do not."

Gordon paced before him. Pinched the bridge of his nose before he swore beneath his breath and said, "You ken I bloody well can't protect me own borders."

Malcolm frowned. "Then we shall continue our agreement. Our stewards will take care of all transactions. Heed me well, Gordon. Rossalyn and Mairi are under my protection."

The laird remained silent, most likely contemplating a different path to getting what he wanted without relinquishing his food stores. Or a plot to slay Malcolm and his men and then take over the keep. 'Twas more likely the latter than the former, if the man were to remain true to character.

His wife came beside him and slipped her hand into his. "Mairi and I are Sutherlands now, Father. You will never attempt to take us from the keep."

Bravo, my wife. He was so proud of her. Aye, he detected a slight tremor in her voice, but her strength also rang true. She was facing the enemy who'd killed her husband and made her life hell. The man who'd leveraged his only granddaughter to gain his boon. She was brave, his wife.

Love filled him, so fully, it momentarily shocked him at its power.

He wanted her. Badly. But now was not the time to ravish his beautiful bride. Later, after her father departed and headed back to the hovel he called a home—then he'd show her how much he loved her.

Gordon inspected them, and if their unity surprised them, he didn't show it. The clock on the mantel clicked away the seconds and then the minutes. He finally nodded. "Aye. The stewards will take care of all transactions."

"Wise choice," Malcolm replied.

"You'll not threaten my family again, Father. Pledge now that you'll not do so."

He nodded.

"Say the words," she insisted.

Taken aback, Gordon grimaced, then said, "Aye, I will not threaten your family again." While he lacked sincerity, Malcolm had to assume the man would do as he said.

If not, he'd feel the wrath of the Sutherland clan.

"Now, I will escort you to your steed and you will leave my land."

"Och, Sutherland. You could offer a man a bit of the drink before you kick 'em out."

"Nay, Father," Rossalyn answered for him. "I'm certain you've enough drink tethered to your saddle."

Malcolm chuckled. Aye, she had spirit, his wife.

"Fine daughter you are," Gordon muttered as he quit the chamber.

"Remain here," Malcolm cautioned his wife. "I'll be back in a thrice."

He had to ensure the bastard left the keep and was headed back to Gordon territory. For the safety of his wife and Mairi and the safety of his clan. If he let his guard down now, 'twould lead to tragic circumstances.

They strode through the main hall, the clansmen regarding them with leery eyes. Laird Gordon had come to the keep with treachery on his mind and Malcolm kenned many knew the man was a bastard just by looking at him and his scowling face.

"'Tis a dire day when a father isn't welcome in his daughter's home."

Malcolm grabbed him by the scruff of the neck and led him to the bailey. "When the father threatens the daughter and his granddaughter, och, 'tis no wonder why the man isn't welcome."

As they approached the gate, Gordon's men slipped off their horses and drew their swords.

"Tell them all is well."

Gordon held up his hands. "Easy, lads. 'Tis naught wrong." He accepted his steed's reins from one of his men. "We'll be leaving this eve, we will."

"M'laird, what about your daughter?"

Malcolm crossed his arms before his chest. "She'll remain here, as will Mairi."

One of Gordon's men came forward with his sword raised and intent clear on his taut features. "You'll no be keeping m'lady and her daughter."

Gordon pushed the man beside. "Don't be daft, Sean. The lass has wed Sutherland. This is where she will stay."

Malcolm was surprised by Gordon's words, but pleased he realized Rossalyn would not be leaving the keep.

"M'laird?" the man growled.

"Let it be, Sean."

Sean hesitated, then skulked away like a beaten dog.

"Off with you, Gordon," Malcolm said. "If word is to be sent, contact my steward."

He nodded, called out to his men to mount up. With one last look at the keep, Gordon clucked to his steed and rode away.

"Think he can be trusted?" Cam asked as he came out of the shadows. Malcolm kenned the man was about. 'Twas Cam's nature to have his back.

"Nay, but don't tell my wife I said so." The thunder of hoofbeats eased and he could no longer see the Gordon clansmen.

Time would only tell if the bastard was going to keep his word. For now, they'd increase the guards and limit time outside the palisade walls.

"And what will you do with Fiona?"

Bollocks. He'd nearly forgotten. 'Twas a difficult position he was in. Fiona was a childhood friend, one he'd cared for like the sister he'd never had. He loathed that he'd hurt her. But her actions were worse than his. Malcolm rubbed the back of his neck and thought on what to do about the lass.

He glanced at the keep and saw the light burning in his chamber. 'Twas late and cold. All he could think of was being in his wife's arms. "She can wait until the morrow."

Cam chuckled. "If I had a wife who looked like yours, I'd say the same thing."

Malcolm slapped him on the back. "Good eve to you. And keep an eye on Fiona to ensure she doesn't leave the keep."

"Aye, Laird. Say goodnight to your lady and Mairi."

"My wife has no need of your goodnights, Cam," Malcolm countered with a grin.

Cam mocked a salute. "Aye, m'laird."

Chapter 13

Rossalyn checked on Mairi, happy to see the lass fed and warm and tucked within her bed. She stood at the window as her father and his men rode off, and prayed 'twould be the last time she saw him. 'Twas a wretched thing to pray about, but the man had caused her so much pain, she wanted nothing more to do with him.

Her husband stood near the gate talking to Cam. Och, two fine men who did well to protect their clan.

She worried about their fate, the fate of the clan and dealing with such a man as her father. But she trusted her husband and his men to ensure nothing else would happen to her or Mairi. She bit at her lip, wondering what sort of fate awaited the woman Fiona. If she understood gossip about the keep correctly, Fiona had been in love with Malcolm and envisioned them marrying. Poor lass and her broken heart.

Easy for Rossalyn now, to ken how it was to love Malcolm—hot, potent, surely all-consuming. If a woman with Fiona's gumption loved Malcolm, 'twas with her body and soul—and would be hard to be denied. Rossalyn determined to request her husband not judge Fiona too harshly.

When Malcolm headed toward the keep, she quickly stoked the fire and slipped out of her gown, leaving her fine, linen chemise on.

Should she be in bed? Would Malcolm consider her brazen? No matter, they were wed and she could think of nothing more that she wanted to do than lay abed with her husband.

A knock sounded on the door. "Wife, may I come in?"

She laughed. "Aye, husband." How wonderful the words felt on her tongue. Shivers of excitement raced through her.

Malcolm entered; closed and locked the door. A wicked grin curled his mouth. As he paced toward her, he lifted his liene over his head, slipped off the belt holding his tartan, and let the cloth fall to the ground.

A magnificent man stood before her. Hard planes of muscles bunched as he walked. Long legs, broad shoulders.

She quivered as her womb clenched. Heat filled her at the intensity of his gaze. How she wanted this man.

How she loved this man.

She swallowed as he stood beside the bed. She whipped back the covers to welcome him in.

"You are wearing too much clothing."

She chuckled. "I think you can remedy that."

With his strong hands he started unlacing her chemise. "Hurry."

He leaned down, still standing beside the bed, and whispered kisses along her bosom. With one swift movement, Malcolm gripped her chemise and tore it down the middle.

"Malcolm," she chastised, though she laughed.

He knelt next to the bed and swept his gaze over her. "You are so very beautiful, my love."

She blushed beneath his scrutiny. "Come to me."

He grinned and said, "As you wish, my love."

Rossalyn canted her head to the side. "'Tis the second time you called me your love."

Malcolm slipped into bed and lay beside her. He tipped up her chin and grazed her lip with the pad of his thumb. His dark eyes held tenderness. "Because you are my love. I love you, Lady Rossalyn Sutherland."

Tears tickled the back of her throat. "You do?"

"Aye." He swept a kiss against her mouth. "I love how you protect our daughter." He kissed the tip of her nose. "I love how you care for the people of my clan. Our clan." He kissed her eyelids. "I love how you have given yourself to me. Given your heart to me."

"Oh, Malcolm." She circled her arms around his neck. "Thank you for sharing your love with me."

He kissed her, brought her tight against him. His flesh singed hers as they made love. Truly made love, their hearts as one as they ravaged each other.

"Malcolm," she cried as passion overwhelmed her. Each part of her body longed to touch his, be touched by him. He consumed her as she met his thrusts. She smoothed her hands over his body, loved when he trembled and groaned in his passion.

Her husband. The man who loved her.

He buried himself deep within her. Rossalyn cried out as her body soared to such pleasurable heights. Malcolm growled as he spilled his seed within her.

"I love you," he whispered after he collapsed next to her.

After a while, light filtered into the chamber, spilling over the furniture and reaching the bed.

Malcolm rose and pulled Rossalyn with him.

He wrapped a blanket around them as they stood before the window.

She smiled, lifted to her toes, and kissed him. "Look, Malcolm."

A full moon filled the night sky—'twas brilliant.

"'Tis the Christmas moon, m'laird." She gripped his hand and held it to her heart. "Beneath the Christmas moon I have found love."

His heart hammered against her hand. Aye, she realized—'twas the truth of it.

"Aye," he echoed. "Love beneath the Christmas moon."

BOOK TWO

HIS BY CHRISTMAS

Chapter 1

"You kenned he'd be vexed."

Fiona Sutherland rolled her eyes heavenward, then glared at the man who was forever scolding her. As if everything Cameron Munro did was perfect.

She grabbed her *arisaid*, whipped it over her shoulders, and headed toward the bailey. Thick, white flakes of snow fell and tangled in her lashes. She ignored the blasted weather and kept walking.

Despite the blanket of snow, heavy footsteps pounded after her.

"What do you have to say for yourself, Fiona?"

She spun to face Cam and fisted her hands at her waist. Anger flared quickly as her heart ratcheted against her chest. She wasn't daft. She kenned exactly what she did. Just as she kenned there'd be consequences. "Aye, the mighty Cam has spoken. Do you think I have to listen to you?"

Cam stared at her with those dark eyes of his. Unreadable, impenetrable. He might be the Sargent-at-Arms for the clan, but he had no place yelling at her. "Why did you lie to the Laird?"

Why, indeed?

Especially since she kenned 'twas wrong. Och, why did she allow her anger to rule her tongue? Truly, she didn't ken who she was when she spat at Malcolm and then talked Lady Rossalyn into fleeing the keep. And she put the lass Mairi in danger as well. Just thinking of it made her want to lose the contents of her stomach. She'd been so vile.

She tugged her fingers through her hair and sighed. Fiona had loved Malcolm Sutherland since she was just a wee lass. He was strong, loyal, and had the most beautiful face she'd ever seen. When his parents died and he became laird, she kenned he'd need a wife. Determined to be the next Lady Sutherland, she would do so with such grace, the clan would revere her. 'Twas something she'd dreamed of for years. They'd rule the clan together and what beautiful bairns they'd make.

When he'd asked Trina to marry him, Fiona kenned 'twouldn't last. She'd seen Trina with another and told the woman to confess or she'd go to Mal. After Trina was banished, Fiona pinned all of her hopes and dreams on Mal, anticipating his proposal.

But now, her dreams were dashed. He'd brought the woman and her child from Clan Gordon—and to make matters worse, he'd wed her.

He'd wed another woman.

Her stomach dropped at the memory of seeing the lady, all refined and beautiful even with the dust from the trail upon her. 'Twas why she'd mocked the woman. Mal was hers and this wench had stolen him.

And when the lovely wee lass appeared, och, Fiona's heart careened. She longed for a husband and a bairn of her own. And now Mal had a wife and daughter. He'd not need her.

Again, her dreams were shattered, for she knew Malcolm would never forsake a promise to his new wife if a child was involved. Mayhap, even without the child. For Laird Sutherland was a fiercely loyal man and once he pledged a promise, 'twould take God himself to force him to break it.

Even as she kenned this about him, the idea he'd forgotten their pledge surprised her. Aye, 'twas a promise made between a lad and lass, but she'd lived with the idea of marriage in her mind and heart ever since. Och, now her heart was shattered.

"Well, Fiona?"

She glanced up and saw Cam glaring at her. Such a large man, with shoulders so braw he blocked some of the falling snow. His jaw clenched and his brow pulled into a straight line. She frowned, not wanting this man to discover why she was so vexed and why she'd tried to force the new Lady Sutherland to leave. Though the reason should be obvious to him. Mal was her love and should be her husband. "'Tis none of your concern. We are no longer young lads and lasses in a time where you and Malcolm order me around."

She jerked when he gripped her arm. "Let go of me," she said with a sneer and a bit of fright at the fierceness of his scowl. Mayhap too strong of a word to describe her feelings. But it seemed as if he'd become larger, more powerful, as he stood peering down at her.

The sheer magnitude of the man left her a little breathless with those black eyes and such fury pulsing around him. She shook her head. Nay, it was only Cam, she reasoned. The same lad she rode across the glen and fished with over the years.

However, 'twas obvious why Mal had him leading the men. He was strong, commanding, and as he clenched his jaw—intimidating. "Leave Lady Sutherland alone. If m'laird has a mind to, you may find yourself out of the keep."

She scoffed, but her pulse ratcheted against her chest. "Mal would never force me from the keep."

Cam shrugged, but released her. "That is to be seen. If you threaten his lady, he may have no choice."

He turned from her and strode toward the stables. Fiona rubbed her arm and kept her gaze on him. He'd a cocksure swagger, truth be told. Long, muscle-bound legs and broad shoulders. He was braw, aye, but not the man Malcolm Sutherland was.

Her Mal.

How was she to live without him? Knowing he was with another woman, in her arms each night and them loving each other, killed her.

Fiona wiped away tears of frustration as her heart broke again. Soon it would be so shattered, it might never heal. She'd end up a shrew. Turning, she continued to make her way outside the keep's wall. A long walk was in order, despite the snow and cold. Pulling her worn *arisaid* tight around her, she braved the wintery conditions.

She kicked at the snow as she paced along the barren landscape until she reached the wee forest. 'Twas too late in the eve to venture inside the dark depths; regardless, she kept walking. An owl hooted and the branches rustled in the wind. She frowned and cursed Laird and Lady Sutherland.

"Why?" Fiona muttered. "Why couldn't he have chosen me?"

She'd been so excited when she'd seen Mal traveling toward the keep, she had urged her mare into a gallop. He'd finally returned and completed his goal of securing food stores. Now he'd be ready and willing to marry. Willing to marry her, she kenned it. Her heart had raced just as she pushed her mare toward the caravan.

While she kenned Mal would be pleased to see her, spying the other woman had sent warnings to her brain and heart.

"You'll catch your death."

She gasped and turned toward the voice. Cam leaned against a grand pine. He crossed his arms before his chest and stared her. Damn, the man was always watching her.

'Twas disconcerting.

"Can't you find another lass to vex?" she taunted. "Or have you worn out your welcome in their beds?"

He chuckled when she wanted him to snarl. "Jealous?" he drawled in that lazy way he had. The man just had a manner about him. She angled her head and studied him. Steady, to be sure or he wouldn't be the Sargent-at-Arms. Loyal; Cam and Mal had been friends since they were born, it seemed. And if she were forced to admit it, aye, he was handsome with those dark eyes, equally dark hair, and chiseled features. And he usually had several lasses swooning when he was near. Many a fight had broken out in the kitchens over who was to serve the man his meals.

He pushed from the tree and strode toward her. His bulky height seemed larger in the outer shadows of the forest. "I'll escort you back to the keep."

Tired and grumpy, she merely nodded. Pacing outside the keep hadn't made her thoughts any clearer. She struggled to hide the fact her teeth were chattering as she tightened her *arisaid* around her.

"Quiet evening."

Her brow furrowed. "'Twould be if you ceased speaking."

He chuckled. "Ah, Fiona lass, such a honeyed tongue."

She glanced up at the sky as snowflakes trickled down toward her through the brightness of the moon.

Cam walked beside her, now silent since she'd not taken his bait. Why did the man irritate her so? She'd kenned him for so long, yet he'd never vexed her as much as he did at this moment.

And now that he'd stopped speaking, she loathed the quiet. If she could, she'd have people and dancing around her at all times. When she was alone, 'twas when she questioned why Mal hadn't turned to her when his parents died or why he hadn't taken her with him as he searched for food stores for the clan. Mostly, why he brought another woman . . . a stranger, no less, to their keep and clan.

"He loves her, you ken this?"

Fiona's heart clenched. Pain sharpened with each breath. 'Twas the truth of it, aye, she kenned. The way Mal looked at Lady Sutherland, passion and desire was banked in his eyes, and when he was with her bairn, 'twas sweet and enviable. Too much for Fiona to bear.

She swallowed, burgeoning tears blurring her vision. "He barely knows her," she managed to say.

Cam slipped his hand beneath her elbow, his palm warm, even through the wool of her *arisaid*. "Watch your step."

Enough.

She ripped from his grasp. "Stop coddling me. I'm not one of those weak women who moons over a man."

He flashed a smile and creases pierced his cheeks— damn him and his dimples. "Aren't you?"

She leveled him with one of her most vile glares. "I'll continue on my own, if you don't mind."

Cam stepped aside and bowed toward her. "Ah, lass, I don't mind at all."

Fiona trudged through the deep snow, past the palisade. She quickly glanced over her shoulder and saw Cam following her at a distance.

What she wouldn't give for the man to leave her alone.

And what she wouldn't give to have Mal's love.

Both, she feared, were impossible.

Ah, she was going to be worth the wait. A strong lass, beautiful, to be sure. But stubborn and in love with the wrong man. Cam observed her striding into the keep, her back ramrod straight and her shoulders square. She'd occupied his thoughts and dreams for too many years.

He'd held back from trying to woo her. Mostly out of respect for his laird. He'd kenned Fiona thought she was in love with Malcolm and this threw a particular wrinkle into his plan. If he'd pressed his case too soon, Fiona would have spurned him as she waited for Malcolm to forsake his lady. Which he'd never do.

Now was the perfect time.

Cam wanted her for his wife.

He wanted her to be the mother of his bairns.

And he wanted her to warm his bed until he drew his last breath.

How to convince her? The woman had been enamored with Malcolm since she could toddle about. Cam'd stood by, watching and waiting until she realized Mal was not enamored of her.

'Twas wretched how she'd been hurt. He'd witnessed her shock, how those green, green eyes had filled with tears and then disbelief. Ah, her legionary ire flashed as bright as fire. Words whipped from her tart tongue and then she was racing back to the keep. He'd been there for her. Had waited for her to see that loving him was a possibility. And still she pined for Mal.

Cam had been patient, too patient.

But now, his restraint was gone.

Mal was wed, and there was no reason for Fiona to continue to moon over him and profess a love which had never been returned.

He'd have to court her without her realizing he was doing so. With her stubborn nature and keen intellect, she'd discover his plan and he'd be thwarted.

Cam entered the keep just in time to see Fiona headed toward the stairs leading to her chamber. Her skirt slipped and he eyed her shapely calf, creamy skin he wagered would be smooth to the touch.

Och, he'd have to control himself.

"Cam," his man Timothy called, "come and quench your thirst."

Ah, a distraction from the lovely Fiona. He eyed the group of men, some already deep in their cups. Their company was a poor substitute for her beautiful face, but he'd no choice in the matter. At least for now.

He accepted the tumbler of whiskey and took a long draw, the liquid sliding down and settling into his stomach.

If it took all night, he'd quench not only his thirst, but his desire for the red-haired vixen.

Chapter 2

Cam woke with a plan to woo Fiona.

It smarted how he had to woo her when any other lass he'd pursued came willing and eager. Since he'd caught the eye of his first lass years ago, all he had to do was beckon and a comely woman would be his for the night. Not that he was a bastard toward women. But he was a man after all, and since Fiona kept him at bay, he enjoyed his share of conquests. Women were a mystery to him, but he loved exploring and savoring all shapes and sizes. Soft skin. Luscious curves. Eyes that glittered with desire. And when he tangled his fingers in their tresses and inhaled, och, it sent desire straight to his cods.

How he loved the scent of a woman.

No matter the dalliances of his past, his mind and heart belonged only to Fiona. And he had to let her subtly ken his feelings.

He rubbed sleep from his eyes and headed to break his fast. After training the men and ensuring the protection of the clan's territory, his time would be limited. And his laird might send other duties his way, as he was wont to do. But all he could think about was Fiona.

The gentle slope of her neck, the vibrant red of her hair, those shiny green eyes, her fiery spirit—all consumed him. Ever since they were young, she'd captivated him. Och, she was intelligent, often teaching him a thing or two. Her wit and biting tongue might send other lads running, but to him, 'twas what made her who she was.

And who he loved.

Cam dressed and secured his sword to his belt. He tethered his hair with a leather strap and pulled on his boots.

One quick glance about his chamber and he frowned, then left in search of food.

He didn't ken why his chamber bothered him. Barren, with hard surfaces save the coverlet on his bed. Bare chest of drawers and flooring. No comfort. 'Twas no sign he belonged and it lacked the touch of a woman. Aye, Mal's chamber had warmth, trinkets strewn about, Mairi's doll and wooden horse before the fire, and the faint scent of feminine soap lingered ever so slightly.

He'd lived in the keep since he was but a wee lad and his father had been felled when his clan aided the Sutherlands during a clan skirmish. His mother had died during his birth, and he certainly didn't have anyone to call family. 'Twas why he'd shadowed Malcolm when they were lads and proved his way through training and fighting and until he was named Sargent-at-Arms.

And now Mal was married. More bairns would come. He'd rely on Cam more and more to protect the clan and Mal's soon to be growing family.

Och, a family—how he wanted what his friend had.

Guilt settled in Cam's gut over his envy.

Laird Sutherland had lost just as much as he had. His parents both gone, although he'd had been lucky to have them longer than Cam. And Mal had the responsibility of the clan, securing their borders and now Laird Gordon's, too. Not to mention feeding a clan the size of Sutherland Keep and at times their Sept clans, those who were tied through family and alliances to the Sutherlands. Worse, Mal had to agree to a deal in which they depended on the veracity of a man like Gordon—a bastard, to be sure.

Cam wore his duties proudly and was loyal only to the Sutherland and the Sept clans. And if his laird asked him to go to the border between Gordon and Sutherland territories, he'd do it in a thrice. 'Twas what he owed the man and the family who'd helped him after he'd lost his father.

And while he owed them, he also needed to do something for himself. Having Fiona as his wife would certainly make him the happiest of men. He wanted a family of his own; surely no one would begrudge him such.

He entered the bustling, main hall and searched for something to start the courting process. Since he'd never had to woo a lass before, he'd have to elicit help with any romantic machinations.

Ah, the perfect person walked into the room.

"Cam. Good morn to you," Brae greeted.

He smiled at the kindly woman and bade her sit. A frown settled between her brows.

"'Tis nothing to be afraid of, Brae. I'm in need of your help."

She grinned and nodded. "Get on with it, I havena' all day."

Such a feisty woman. She'd run the kitchens and serving lasses since he could remember. Fair, but strict she was, assuring the clan's ability to make do with wretched crop yields. When Mal's father died, Brae was the one who'd approached with the news of the dwindling food stores.

"I want to woo a wife."

She tipped her head back and laughed. "You'll not be needing my help with that, lad. Why, I could go in the kitchen and announce you're looking for a wife and the lasses would run me down trying to get to you."

He chuckled, relaxed in his chair, and crossed his arms over his chest. "I want to woo Fiona."

Abruptly, Brae sobered and then her eyes widened. "Fiona," she exclaimed with wonder and a bit of surprise. "Are you certain, lad?"

He grinned. Fiona had earned her contrary reputation honestly. "Aye."

"Well." That single word held a heavy dose of skepticism. "'Twill be tricky. She's hurting and not likely to receive your attention. She'll refuse you if you push her."

Aye. Fiona was an independent woman, but with a vulnerability about her and something painful in her gaze that resulted from more than Mal's so-called betrayal. Cam had witnessed it too many times. When those green eyes turned sad, it broke his heart. For her soul was strong and if sadness lingered, 'twas a grievous wound within her.

"Lad, you'll have to go slowly." A quick smile flashed on Brae's aged face. "Little things. Things a lass such as Fiona would appreciate. Nothing obvious."

Aye, from what he knew of Fiona, she wouldn't want a gift-giving swain made public. "Could you send a meal to her chamber as a courtesy?"

Brae's smile forced her wrinkles to crease around her eyes. "For certain, Cam. 'Tis a kind gesture." She patted his arm and relayed his desire to one of the kitchen lasses.

His wooing would need to be quick, for if Fiona discovered his plan she'd fight him *and* the desire he kenned she'd have for him if she just gave him a chance.

Aye, he'd court her, gently but swiftly, for he'd only a fortnight.

And she'd be his by Christmas.

"Fiona, lass," someone called from the hallway.

Fiona pulled a pillow over her head. The knocking persisted. "Ugh," she grunted as she tossed the pillow aside. Squinting at the bright morning light, she propped herself on her elbows.

Who the devil would wake her so early?

She plopped back onto the mattress and buried her face in her pillow to ward off the sunlight.

"Fiona?" the voice grew testy. "I havena all day, lass. 'Tis duties I have."

"Come in," she mumbled into the pillow.

"Get up, lass." Una, one of the cooks, bustled into her chamber with a swirl of purpose. "I was asked to bring you a tray."

She frowned as she tossed the pillow aside and sat up. "Why?"

"Och, I don't ken. Something about a man wishing you to start your day right."

Fiona bit at her lip. "What man?" Her mind reeled. Had Mal reconsidered? Was there hope?

Una set the tray on her bed and shook her finger at Fiona. "Does it matter? You're breaking your fast in your chamber instead of a noisy hall."

Aye, but it did matter, greatly. It mattered if she'd allow herself an inkling of hope.

"Now get your arse up, eat your food, and then go to Brae. She's something for you to do."

Brae was forever bossy, but Fiona did have a soft spot for the auld woman. She'd taught her a good thing or two as she'd grown. And since Fiona's parents were gone, Brae had taken her under her wing.

The aroma of the salty bacon enticed, and Fiona picked up a rasher as Una moved about her chamber, trying but failing to look as if she weren't being nosey. 'Twas obvious the woman was trying to linger enough to get out of serving in the hall. A boisterous clan like the Sutherlands made for chaotic mealtimes and a busy kitchen.

Fiona didn't envy the lasses who had meal duty. Being stuck in a hot kitchen would drive her to distraction. And while her duties were sometimes laborious, she had the freedom to move about the keep as she pleased.

Una slanted her head to the side and gazed at her with shrewd eyes. "'Tis grand news our laird has taken a wife." She slid her hand along the chest of drawers, then peered at her fingers. Una would not find a speck of dust in her chamber.

Fiona paused mid-bite. Her hand shook as she set the bacon down and glared at Una. "What's so grand about it?" she demanded with wavering control.

Una folded Fiona's *arisaid* and set it upon the chest of drawers. "A nasty hole." She fingered the rent in the woolen material.

Aye, and the tear had been earned when Fiona raced back to the keep after Malcolm introduced his new bride.

She fumed at the cook. "Answer my question."

Una crossed her arms across her bosom and glared back. "You're vexed because you always thought he'd be yours, but the rest of us kenned otherwise."

Swallowing the bile rising in her throat, Fiona shifted restlessly. "He *was* to be mine."

Una softened her stance and stretched out a hand as sympathy filled her gaze. "Men tend to make decisions without asking us. But ken this, he loves you like a sister, no more. He's always told you as such. But you're too stubborn to listen."

Fiona shook her head in denial. "No."

They'd vowed to wed when they were children. Aye, they were wee, but there was a pledge because he'd promised to always be there for her, always take care of her. As they grew, she and Mal—Cam, too—plotted, played, and worked side by side. Mal filled her memories with happiness and love. And now he had another, sharing his days. His nights.

Her gut clenched anew at the idea of Mal in another woman's arms.

Then she sighed. "Tell Brae I'll be down in a thrice."

Una waited for a moment, her gaze tight on Fiona, before she turned and left the chamber.

Pushing the food aside, Fiona rose from her bed. Who was the fool who'd sent her the tray? Surely Mal wouldn't care, now that he had a wife.

No matter. Chores awaited about the keep.

She pulled her hair into a respectable knot at the base of her neck and riffled through her clothing for something clean to wear.

The image of Lady Rossalyn came to mind, elegant and beautiful whether she wore a gown or serviceable skirt and *liene*. Next to her, Fiona felt like a bumbling lass. She raised a frown to the ceiling and heaved another sigh. She'd never been at a loss for bravado and now this new woman had put her on the defense.

After securing a dark wool skirt about her waist and tugging on a clean enough *liene*, she fled her chamber determined to find Brae and ignore the new lady and her bairn. Not to mention Mal and Cam. Soon, she'd be avoiding the entire keep.

Mal had yet to talk to her about what she'd done, or reveal what type of punishment he'd dictate. She shivered at the thought of having a conversation with him. A wretched conversation which included his wife and new lass. She inhaled sharply. Why did she act so rashly? Why?

As she trotted down the staircase, her heart lurched at the sight of Malcolm standing near the laird's table as he pointed to the grand tree in the main hall.

If only he'd smile at her that way.

The wee lass, Mairi, clapped her hands. Mal reached down and lifted her upon his broad shoulders. Mairi kissed him on the head and if possible, his smile grew.

Fiona clutched her chest. 'Twas heart wrenching to watch.

The lass babbled as they strode to the tree. Lady Rossalyn approached from across the room and touched Mal's arm.

The woman wore the clan tartan across her chest. Aye, she'd already become one of them. Fiona had never felt so useless.

Mal gave his new wife a soft smile and she returned his grin with a brilliant one of her own. There was no mistaking the look they shared. This was a couple in love.

She clutched her stomach and slipped from the hall, out the back of the keep. Brae's chores could keep until later and Fiona already kenned what the woman wanted her to do. 'Twas what she did every day.

Despite the despair nearly choking her, she found her way to Helen's crofter. Caring for others would be a way to distract her from her broken heart. The auld woman had been sickly as of late and Fiona would see if she could help. She knocked on the door and heard a muffled plea to enter.

"Good day to you, Helen."

Smoke assailed her as she entered the dark crofter.

"Fiona, me lass. 'Tis lovely to see you."

Even with her heart aching, Fiona smiled at the woman's greeting. Helen sat in her chair by the fire with a shawl about her shoulders. Her grin lit her face. 'Twas a shame she lived alone, for Helen was a grand woman with many stories to tell.

Fiona propped the door open and moved to the fireplace. 'Twould need to be examined at by one of the men. Fiona caught her lip between her teeth. *Unless I climb upon the roof meself and clean the stack.*

Would she be able to manage? Aye, she was a strong lass. She didn't need a man to help her with her duties.

"'Tis a bit of wood outside if you'll be wanting to stoke the fire."

Dear God, 'twas nearly boiling in the crofter as it was.

"Nay, Helen. 'Tis a bit of cleaning I'm up to. Did you break your fast?"

The woman flapped a hand and said, "Aye, don't be worrying."

Fiona grabbed an apron from the peg on the wall and started tidying the small crofter. Poor Helen had lost her husband a few years ago and didn't have any living children to help her in her dotage. Fiona did what she could, but she wasn't able to visit as much as she would like.

"I'll gather some fresh water." She found the bucket knocked over in the kitchen. "Och, Helen. Have you been without water since I was here last?" With all of the drama of Lady Rossalyn's arrival, it had been several days since she'd visited Helen's crofter.

The auld woman cast her gaze to the floor and fingered her shawl. "Not as long as that, my dear. I tripped over it yester eve."

As the woman's gaze failed to meet hers, Fiona doubted 'twas just the eve before. She knelt before Helen and gripped one of her wrinkled hands. Helen met her gaze. "Next time, tie a handkerchief on the door latch as I showed you."

Tears rimmed Helen's rheumy eyes and she lifted shaking fingers to pat Fiona's face. She was a large-boned woman, strong in her youth, but her pride was the problem. She didn't like accepting help. Fiona saw it each and every time she aided her. 'Twas why she asked advice or guidance with even the most menial of chores. Truth be told, Helen had taught her so many things.

"'Tis a grand lass you are, Fiona dear. You do well by your parents."

She gave a wry smile. Aye, she'd done well by them and here she was, husbandless and bairnless at her ripening age, taking care of the elder clan members. She loved them all and never regretted her duty. But she was lonely, her nights becoming long and cold. And her heart . . . her heart needed tending and someone to love. With Mal wed, such love might never come her way.

"'Tis a pleasure to help you, Helen." With a quick glance about the crofter, Fiona noticed there was little wood for the fire. "I'll gather some water and wood. Then I'll collect some stores for your meals."

Helen patted her arm. "Before you leave, tell me about the new lady. 'Tis a beauty, I hear."

Fiona rolled her eyes heavenward before she could catch herself.

Helen chuckled, which led into a coughing fit. Fiona patted her back until the fit eased.

"I'll fetch some honey as well."

As she tried to walk away, Helen gripped her hand. "Lass, will she be a fine lady for our laird?"

The word "nay" nearly leapt from her mouth. With a sigh, Fiona nodded. She kenned Mal and knew he'd never forsake his wife for another. Especially a wife on whom he bestowed such desired-filled glances.

Helen grinned as she patted Fiona's hand. "Grand. 'Tis grand news."

Scowling as she left the crofter in search of wood and water, Fiona thought about the times she and Malcolm were inseparable. Riding across the glen, hiding from Malcolm's father when they'd done something vexing, and sneaking tarts from the larder. Their escapades had lessened as they'd grown and Mal's responsibilities expanded. Now, they'd cease altogether. With a deep breath, she headed toward the well.

"Early to work, I see."

Fiona stilled, then continued forward. "Aye, as I am every day."

He didn't follow her, but she felt Cam's gaze upon her as if he were actually touching her skin. Heat rushed over her face. She rubbed the back of her neck, vexed the man affected her so. He'd never bothered her before but now, och, Cam was such an annoyance.

"Are you aiding Auld Helen, then?"

"Aye," she called over her shoulder. Didn't the man see her leave Helen's crofter with a bucket in her hand? *Men be daft.*

"A helpful lass, you are."

Helpful? Anger filled her. 'Twas how folk viewed her, but there was so much more to her. And she never had the chance to show people. The men saw her as one of their own and the women tended to shy away from her. Mal always said it was because she was so beautiful the women were jealous, but she doubted it. There were many just as pretty as she was, more so. The new lady of the keep, for one.

She ignored Cam, hooked the bucket on the rope, and cranked until it dipped into the water. Mayhap she should gather two buckets. With the state of the clan and Gordon's unexpected arrival and quick departure, one never kenned if more excitement was on its way.

She set the bucket to the side and headed toward the kitchen in search of another, finding one that would suit.

"Una, could you bring food for Auld Helen?"

Una grinned and waved from across the kitchen. "After I've seen to the midday meal."

"Enough for a few days, if you'd please."

The cook smiled. "'Tis kind you are, Fiona."

Heat flushed her cheeks. 'Twas no bother to her. The woman had been like a grandmother to her and she loved her fiercely.

Just as she had a soft spot for many of the elderly in the clan. When she was a lass, she'd follow the older folk about the keep. Her mother was forever looking for her and more often than not, Fiona was tucked on the lap of one of the elder women, listening to a story. How she loved the slight, aged timber of their voices, their enthusiasm, how much pleasure it seemed to give them to share with her. When she'd look up at them, their wrinkled faces would brighten and they'd laugh and chat with her. It warmed her to think of it and she renewed her pledge not to let them go without.

After she gathered the buckets of water, she strode to Helen's crofter. And stopped short.

"What the devil are you doing?"

Cam halted his axe mid-swing. Sweat glistened on his brow and dampened his *liene*. Her mouth gaped before she could stop herself.

A slow smile creased his face. "Chopping wood, lass."

The water sloshed over the side of the bucket, wetting her skirt. She plunked them down and crossed her arms before her chest. "'Tis my duty, not yours."

"I wished to help." He wiped the glistening sweat from his brow. Och, how his intense inspection vexed her as he trailed his gaze from her dusty shoes to her face. His smile widened. 'Twas disarming how his dimples made him so charming and handsome when she wanted to loathe him.

She was at a loss of what to say as the low morning sun haloed his form. Tall, strong, aye he had a way about him, with his broad forehead and straight nose. His mouth often curved into a wide grin.

As he continued to assault the wood, Fiona stared, thinking if she glared at him long enough he'd vanish.

But the longer she kept an eye on him, the more she was reminded of their youth, when they raced the horses wildly across the glen. Mal was more competitive and would ride his steed into the ground to beat them. Cam would graciously lose, usually blaming his horse or that he'd eaten too much when he broke his fast, thus riding slower.

Many a time Cam would hang back as if watching over her, while Mal would dash into the distance without a backward glance. Then a warrior yell, sounding throughout the glen, would startle birds into flight.

"Head inside, Fiona," Cam now said. "I'll finish here."

Gathering her wits, she walked around him, maintaining a wide berth. The woodpile was quickly replenished, but the man kept chopping.

"Where next?" he called just before she entered the crofter.

"Auld David, and after, to see Millie." Then she realized what she'd revealed. Her restless sleep had weakened her. "Nay—"

Cam sent her a warning glance that held a bit of fire. Usually an easygoing man, the ire surprised her. "I'll finish what I started."

She huffed a sigh and entered Helen's crofter.

"He's a braw lad, Fiona. You should think about *him*, no' our laird."

She fisted her hands impotently. "Why does everyone need to speak on whom I should think about? The man is merely helping with the wood. 'Tisn't a proposal of marriage."

Blast it, Helen's words festered. She wanted to storm outside and yell at Cam for interfering with her duties once again. 'Twas all she had and she didn't need help.

The dear woman wagged her finger and shook her head as if Fiona had not a wee bit of sense. "Lass, you've a lot to learn about lads."

While Helen had experience, she didn't ken how Cam made her feel when he took it upon himself to complete her duties. As if Fiona failed at yet another thing. The inability to make Malcolm see she was the wife for him ate at her pride. And now a man, who thought she needed help aiding those she cared for nearly every day, was making matters worse.

"Wet the tea and sit a while," Helen said.

Fiona held a sigh. It wouldn't hurt to have tea with Helen. The woman had done so much for her. She ensured the door was open, stoked the fire, then set the water buckets in a safe area, lest Helen trip on them again. After she hung the kettle on the hook near the fire, she gathered some biscuits and set them on the small table.

The thunk of the axe outside seemed to echo in the small crofter, reminding her Cam was still completing *her* chores. She bristled, determined to ignore him.

"Now, my Andrew was a strong lad," Helen started. "And such a handsome man. Och, the lasses chased after him well into our marriage."

Fiona snorted. 'Twas the way of it when there was a handsome man about. "How did you keep them away?"

Helen cackled with laughter. "Weel, with one particular lass, I slapped her face and told her I'd do worse if she dared approach my husband again."

Fiona chuckled, finding it easy to imagine the woman doing such.

"But it didn't matter, you ken. I kept my man happy at home." She wiggled her brows. "If you ken what I mean."

Heat flushed her face. "Aye, Helen. I ken."

At times she wondered if she *could* make a man happy. She might not admit it to others, but Fiona knew of her own contrary and wee bit stubborn nature. *Grumpy*, was what Malcolm used to say. If he'd only shared her love, she'd never be grumpy again.

"Now, lass. Tell me how we're going to find you a husband."

"What?" Fiona abruptly stood. Panic tightened her chest. "I'm not looking for a husband." Now that Mal was wed, there was no other upon which she'd pin her hopes and heart.

"Since the laird is happily wed," Helen shrugged, "you must be looking elsewhere."

Narrowing her gaze, Fiona attempted to determine if the woman was trying to vex her or merely curious. The way she inclined her head to the side as she stirred honey into her tea made Fiona think 'twas only curiosity. But there was a hint of a twinkle in Helen's rheumy gaze. She'd a mischievous sense of humor and when she was younger, Fiona recalled the auld woman playing pranks on her dear friends.

Instead of chastising, Fiona furrowed her brow. "I must see to the others."

Helen chuckled, a mix of rusty laughter and cragged cough. "You can run from me, lass, but you can't run from yourself." She coughed again.

"Be sure to add honey to your tea," Fiona urged as she crossed the threshold. "And if your cough worsens, let me ken."

The woman nodded, but still had a full grin on her face. 'Twould be more mischief from that one, Fiona knew.

Och, the fireplace. As she left the crofter she searched for Cam. He must have tired of cutting wood. Thank God. She found a ladder and dragged it to Helen's home.

After she leaned against the crofter, she slowly made her way up and peered in the chimney. She'd need a broom.

As she started to descend, the ladder slipped. "Och," she cried as she felt herself fall.

"Watch yourself," Cam said as he caught her.

His strong hands steadied her, wrapped around her, held her tight.

Her skin burned from his touch and her heart ratcheted within her chest.

"What the devil, lass? You could have hurt yourself." He held on to her as if he never wanted to let go. His gaze searched her face. "Are you well?"

Her breath caught in her throat. He'd saved her life. Dear God, she hated to think what would have happened if he wasn't there.

"Well?"

"Thank you," she mumbled as her heart settled and stopped pounding against her chest.

He chuckled. "'Tis all you can say?"

Heat infused her as his strong arms tightened around her. She tried to tear her gaze from his dark eyes, but couldn't. They pulled her in with a mix of browns and golds. "You can set me down." Even though she didn't want him to. For the first time in a long while, she felt safe.

He ignored her demand and brought her into Helen's crofter. Then coughed. "I will look at the chimney."

"I can do it."

His brow lifted. "Aye, I saw how you took care of the chimney."

The nerve of the man. "Let me go."

"Lass, are you all right?" Helen asked as she stood and offered the chair.

Cam set her down. "She slipped off the ladder."

Her hand flew to her mouth. "Och, lass." She hobbled over to peer at Fiona. "You should have let the lads take care of it."

"I can do what any lad can."

Helen smoothed Fiona's hair from her face. "I ken. But sometimes we have to let them manage the hard work so they ken they're needed."

Fiona cast her eyes heavenward. "Aye, Helen." Although she didn't believe it. When had she needed a man to help her? Every day, she set out and did what was required for the elders. Chopping wood, cooking meals, wetting tea. There was nothing she wouldn't do for them.

Cam chuckled. "She thinks she can do it all by herself."

Helen swatted Cam. "Aye, she's a strong-minded lass."

"I ken."

"I'm sitting right here!"

They laughed.

"Right you are, Fiona. Stay a bit and let Cam fix the chimney."

Cam eyed her, his gaze unreadable. "I'll be back in a thrice."

She sighed when he left. The man befuddled her and there was a certain discomfort when he was near. 'Twas as if she'd become aware of every breath he took, where his gaze led, and what he was about to say.

'Twas foolish, she kenned, especially since he was so bothersome. Truly, she'd do well to stay away from him.

"Now lass, he's a fine man. A fine man, indeed." Helen tutted as she poured some tea. "If only I were a wee bit younger, I'd set my cap for him and you'd be on his mind no more."

"He has no interest in me." Fiona kept an eye on the door, waiting for it to open, for Cam to enter and say the chimney was fixed.

"No interest, aye? The lad didn't take his eyes from you. When he carried you in here, I thought he was about to ravish you, lass."

"Ravish?" Fiona tried to ignore the squeak in her voice. The woman was losing her mind. Cam was . . . Cam. He had no care for her except to chastise her whenever possible.

The woman grinned. "Aye, when a man has the look of hunger in his eyes, there's only one way to sate it."

"By eating, I assume," she retorted wryly.

Helen laughed and slapped the table. Tea cups rattled against saucers and tea dribbled over the rims. "Och, lass. You're witty."

"So I've been told." Truly the woman must be a bit addled today. Why would she think Cam wanted to ravish her? All he did was save her when she could have been hurt—or worse. He was doing his duty as a clan warrior. He'd do it for anyone who was about to fall to their death.

"Now, you need to let him tend to you, lass. Men like to be needed as I said. It makes them feel manly. And if you've a chance, a wee kiss will encourage the lad."

A kiss? "You're mad."

A soft chuckle eased from the auld woman. "Nay, lass. *You're* mad if you don't want to kiss a lad such as our Cam. He's a fine, fine man."

Heat rushed over her cheeks. *Kiss Cam*? Nay. 'Twould be foolish to even think he'd want to kiss her.

The door eased open. "'Tis finished, Helen."

Fiona glanced about the small crofter and saw the smoke was clearing as the fire drew properly in the fireplace.

"Thank you, Cameron. 'Tis glad I am you saved our fair Fiona and fixed me chimney."

Had he heard what Helen said? Fiona searched his face. Those dark eyes returned her stare, but otherwise didn't reveal anything.

He bowed. "'Tis my pleasure, m'lady."

"Och, go on with you."

Fiona grinned as Helen blushed and tittered like a young lass.

She stood. "I'm off to visit David."

"Fiona, stay a while." Helen patted the table. "We've more to chat about." Her gaze flitted back and forth between Cam and herself.

She'd just bet Helen wanted to chat. More likely, the auld woman plotted to play matchmaker.

Helen sweetened her smile. "Cam, would you like some tea?"

"No, he doesn't," Fiona said as she stood.

His jaw flexed and his black brows pitched downward. He rubbed the back of his neck, yet kept his keen gaze on her. "Don't I?" he challenged. "Seems I've a mind for some tea. Do you have any biscuits, Helen?"

Helen clapped her hands. "Aye. Fiona, fetch the biscuits."

Fetch the biscuits? The woman was determined. She sighed and looked for the biscuits. A quick peek over her shoulder revealed Cam watching her yet again with a bemused grin on his face.

Och, the man—he had no right to stare at her so. His eyes darkened and his mouth quirked up at the corner. His arrogant gaze revealed enjoyment of her discomfort.

She set the biscuits on the table. "I've wood to stack and then I'm off to see David."

"Fiona." Cam's tone held a warning.

"I've duties, Cam. I don't have time for biscuits and tea."

He leaned back onto the chair and crossed his arms before his chest. His dark gaze never left her and guilt shifted up her spine. Aye, she was being a boor. But the man—and Helen, too—pushed her to something she didn't want. Truly feel something she didn't want. Cam wasn't the man for her.

"I'm going to finish stacking the wood." If Cam and Helen spoke of her, she'd hear it and be able to put a stop to it.

Outside Helen's crofter, Fiona grabbed one piece of wood after the other. Stacking them neatly, she was nearly finished when she turned and saw Cam leaning against the doorjamb. He straightened and strode to her with a cocky grin on his face, then held out his hand. She stared as if she didn't ken what he wanted. In truth, she didn't.

"I'll finish the wood."

She frowned and pulled back the piece of wood, cradling it as if holding the sweetest bairn. "No need. Go and train. Play with your sword."

Another step forward and he was close enough to touch. Heat rushed to the spot where his strong forearm brushed against hers. She swallowed and glanced up at him. Tight lines bracketed his broad mouth. She took in the man, the sharp angles of his face, those dark eyes and even darker hair. A lock slipped onto his forehead and he blew it aside.

"Play with my sword, you say?" His husky voice swept over her and nearly curled her toes as she waited for him to say more.

He dragged his finger along her jaw. She flinched, not because she didn't want him to touch her, but because the gentleness surprised her. His eyes narrowed, but before he moved away, she tossed the wood to the ground and gripped his hand.

"Aye, Fiona?" he said as he lifted his brow. The expectation filling his gaze worried her.

She loosened her grip. "I . . . I don't ken."

He laughed. Och, 'twas a sound which wrought grand memories—warm and familiar—of childhood times. Easier times when there wasn't a rift between her and Mal.

She shook her head. "Nothing."

Though he gave a brief nod, she didn't miss the disappointment that flashed in his gaze and tightened his mouth. Her stomach clenched and guilt filled her once again.

"I'll finish here. Go and see Auld David."

His tone was flat and she kenned she'd hurt him. She opened her mouth to say something, offer an apology—anything. But nothing came to mind.

He bent and picked up the wood she'd tossed aside. Then he stacked it and began setting the other pieces.

"Well? Don't you have duties?" His sarcasm wasn't lost on her.

With a sigh Fiona headed to Auld David's crofter.

Chapter 3

He'd give her a few minutes and then bring the wood to the rest of the crofters. Fiona took on too much and rarely, if ever, asked for help. 'Twas a kindness in her others didn't see as often as he'd like. Aye, she could be fierce, but mostly because she was loyal to the core and defended others when the need arose.

Cam glanced at the thatched roof, glad the chimney was clear and Fiona hadn't broken her neck in order to fix it. While she and Helen were talking, their conversation eased up the chimney and reached him. He'd heard their patter—all of it. Their discussion had made him smile. Fiona had a way with the elders; 'twas endearing. And he couldn't help but fall a bit in love with dear Helen for championing his cause.

Even though 'twas obvious Fiona wanted nothing to do with him.

Fiona was like a daughter to the woman, and Helen had often claimed she'd never survive without Fiona's help. Cam had been aware of what she did for the elder clan members. Day after day and sometimes several times a day if one was ill, she'd trek about, bringing food, water, and company to those many had forgotten. The poor souls were bound to their homes, rarely able to venture into the keep and enjoy the festivities of the main hall.

And there she was, striding across the bailey, her glorious, fiery hair swaying in tandem with her hips. Full hips, womanly, and how he itched to slid his hand along her trim waist and over their curve.

He feared Fiona didn't realize what a special woman she was. Strong in spirit and body, kind, gentle if needed, and lovely beyond compare. And she should be cherished—by him.

Her assistance of the clan's elderly warmed his heart. A caring woman would be a caring wife and mother.

If possible, he loved her more because of the selfless acts.

Aye, he loved her—always had.

Just the mere sight of her made his stomach fill with nerves, despite his desire to remain steady. Quite the lad he became when she was near. Sweat ran down his back, he had to restrain all thought of touching her, and when she smiled his heart nearly stopped. The curve of her mouth lit up her face and added a sparkle to her green eyes. Glittering orbs, they were.

If his men learned of his sentimental thoughts, they'd surely throw him from the keep and call him man no more.

Still, he couldn't help wondering if he was worthy in her eyes. Or would she always be comparing him to Malcolm? And Mal was a grand man who led the clan with honor. 'Twould be trying, to be always compared to him.

Cam gathered a load of wood and headed toward Auld David's crofter. The man had been infirm since he'd broken his leg a year past. Fiona was partial to him. And the elder was equally charmed by her. He loved to regale her with tales of years past and always claimed Fiona was his favorite audience.

Lady Rossalyn and Mairi strode past Auld David's crofter toward him. "Good day to you, Cam."

He bowed his head. "And to you, m'lady and Lady Mairi."

"Cam, I'm going to see my pony."

"'Tis a fine day for it, lass."

Mairi jumped up and down, her dark curls bouncing along with her until her mother gently set her hand on her shoulder. Still, the lass wriggled as if it killed her to wait for her mother to head to the stables.

Lady Rossalyn looked questioningly at him. "Where are you headed with your arms loaded with wood?" Her brow lifted.

Surmising she kenned he was supposed to be training the men, Cam flashed what he knew was a most charming smile. "I'm helping fair Fiona."

"And does she welcome your help?"

Cam laughed. "Nay, m'lady." But he wouldn't let that stop him.

Her mouth quirked with a smile. "Good luck to you, Cam."

Lady Rossalyn guided Mairi on their way to the stable. Cam continued to Auld David's crofter.

"Do not take one step closer, Cameron." There she stood with a frown on her face and her chin lifted up in defiance. The haughty tilt sent sunlit flames over her hair as well as a caress along her beautiful face and down her neck. "I mean it."

With a chuckle, he started relieving his burden outside David's door.

"Not so close," she chastised as she picked up each piece he dropped and set them toward the south side of the crofter. "Do you want the man to have another mishap?"

He followed her, noticing the flush of red on her cheeks. She looked so fetching, it took his breath away.

"I can do this myself. Don't I every day?" She continued to fix each piece of wood he stacked, muttering under her breath as she did so. He couldn't help but grin at her frustration.

"Last one."

As she turned to set the final piece of wood on the stack, she tripped right into his arms.

Soft, oh, so soft. Her curves fit perfectly against his body. A sigh slipped past her plump, bowed lips and her green eyes widened with shock and a bit of curiosity. Her tongue darted across her mouth, wetting it.

He couldn't help himself.

Slowly he eased toward her and brushed a kiss against her lips. When she didn't yell or shy away, Cam dove in for more.

Desire coursed, swift and potent. Their lips tangled and he swallowed the sweet moan rumbling from deep within her. He tugged her closer, her full breasts pushing against his chest. Pure agony, as his cods swelled with stark need.

Home, the kiss represented . . . finally, he was home as he threaded his fingers through her hair and her nails dug into the sensitive flesh at the back of his neck. He slipped his tongue into the moist cavity of her mouth.

He could go on tasting her forever.

But she wrenched away from him. Panic filled her eyes as her chest heaved. "Don't ever touch me again." Her hand lifted and the sound of flesh slapping against flesh shocked him.

The lass struck me!

He opened his mouth to say . . . to say anything, yet no words formed. His skin heated and he touched the spot where she hit him as anger surfaced.

Fiona backed up and covered her mouth with both hands. "Cam—I—"

He thrust out a palm to stop her from speaking. "You've made yourself perfectly clear."

Her gaze pitched to the ground.

She'd struck him. 'Twas the first time he'd been struck by a woman and he prayed 'twould be his last.

What should he do? Ignore her? Let her go?

His heart clenched at the thought of losing her.

All of his dreaming, of a wife and bairns, had quickly turned into a nightmare.

"Go," he whispered with as much control as he could muster.

Her face leeched of all color. She turned, but glanced over her shoulder before she darted into the crofter.

Those emerald eyes still mesmerized him as they filled with sadness.

Did she regret her action? If she did, would he forgive such an action?

Dare he pin his future on such a slight indication?

Just before the door closed on the crofter, Fiona looked directly at him. A shimmer of crystalline tears filled her gaze.

Were the tears because she slapped him or because she felt she'd betrayed Mal? Cam kenned the lass held a lingering torch for their laird, but surely she didn't think there was still a flicker of hope? And would she respond so to him if she loved another?

Bollocks. Didn't matter, for she'd slapped him.

He scrubbed a hand over his face. What a wretched mess.

Yet she'd responded to his kiss, pressed herself against him, moaned when he delved for the second time. That little moan, just a moue from her full lips, set fire to his loins as no woman had done before. *She'd* responded to him.

Not Laird Malcolm Sutherland. *To him*.

Aye, mayhap he should risk his future and chance another slap by pursuing her.

For she was the love of his life, 'twas no going back.

His life would be hell without her.

Fiona leaned against the door and blew out a breath. How could she ever make amends?

She'd never raised a hand to another in her life, and now she'd hurt one of her childhood friends. Dear God, she'd struck someone. The clap of flesh against flesh reverberated through her mind. Harsh, even cruel. How could she have acted in such a manner? But . . . but the man had taken liberties. She'd been saving herself for Malcolm and Cam was certainly aware of that love. And even if Mal was no longer part of her future, it didn't give Cam permission to—to kiss her.

Why *did* he kiss her?

Right in the middle of the bailey, where all of the clan could see if they'd a mind to. By the evening meal, word of the kiss would spread. She rubbed her hands along her arms. Truth be told, when his lips had brushed against hers, she'd been shocked. Then tendrils of heat coursed through her and admittedly, curiosity propelled her to allow the kiss to continue. Not only continue, but savor and enjoy and match his enthusiasm with her own.

Desire and such sweetness filled her. He'd been gentle and then . . . then he'd drowned her in a flurry of emotions. Flutters in her stomach, heat through her veins, and och, did her heart actually pound against her chest?

"Lass?"

She opened her eyes and looked at Auld David. The man must think her mad.

As must Cam.

Would he ever forgive her? Then she wondered when she had ever *wanted* Cam to forgive her. Aye, he was a childhood friend, but as a man, he'd barely given her a second glance unless he set himself to chastise her. And now he wouldn't stop following her, *helping* her.

"You're a wee bit flushed, lass."

She gave a sigh. "I'm well." As the man chatted about his various aches and pains, she tidied his crofter and set to making a meal for him.

"Was that Cam?"

Did the auld man hear or see what happened? "Aye, he carried the firewood." She headed toward his table and grabbed a dirty pot. Luckily, he'd water left in the bucket so she could clean it. She'd hate to run into Cam as she fetched more.

David grinned and bobbed his grizzled head. "Such a helpful lad, he is. And braw to boot."

Scrubbing harder, she took her ire out on the pot as if it were her worst enemy. Did every clansman think Cam was a braw lad?

Why had he kissed her? Och, her mind spun with the idea of the gesture and the emotions wrought from his lips against hers. She clutched her chest, wetting her *liene* as she tried to gain control of her thoughts.

Cam was not the man for her.

But which man was? She wanted to love and be loved back. Malcolm was no longer hers for the taking. Her mind kenned this, but her heart still reeled at the idea he'd wed another. How was she to move forward?

She stopped scrubbing and stifled a sob. When had her life become such a mess?

"Lass, the pot is clean."

"Aye, David," she said as she wiped away her pointless tears.

"Come and sit, while I tell you a story."

She suppressed a sigh, then set the pot aside. Collecting tumblers, she filled them with ale for both her and David. When a Highlander had a tale to tell, she kenned 'twould take a wee bit of time.

"I loved many a woman in me day," he said as he waggled his brows. "Beauties, all of them. But none were as lovely as my dear Maggie." After a draw on his ale, he continued, "But I was not the only man who wanted her."

Fiona rested her hand on her chin and listened to the auld man speak. He'd a cocky grin on his face and a bit of a twinkle in his eyes. "Hard to believe there was a woman who could resist you," she teased.

He canted his head to her and winked. "Aye, but resist she did. In fact, she was to wed the other man."

"And you stole her away?"

A coarse chuckle rumbled from the auld man. She tried to see the lad he'd been. But at the wizened age of seventy, 'twas hard to discern. With a craggy face, a few scars across his brow and chin, mayhap he was handsome enough to win a lass away from her intended.

"Stole, such an ugly word," David said with a shrug. "Nay, she was always mine, the other man just wouldn't accept she wasn't his."

'Twas obvious, his motive to tell her such a story. Apparently the entire clan kenned of her love for Mal. Och, hadn't she called him hers since they were just wee bairns? The folk must think her the biggest fool.

"And did he ever accept Maggie was yours?"

David gave a sad shake of his head as he indicated for her to refill his tumbler. "'Tis a bit of a tragedy, lass. The man never recovered and left the keep. We haven't seen him since. 'Tis told he was killed near Inverness. Others say he died a lonely, auld man who never found love."

A shiver chased down her spine. Was his tale a warning? Would she suffer the same fate as the man in his story? Wandering Scotland, never to find love? 'Twasn't the life she saw for herself, alone, without love.

David raised his tumbler. "May those who lose love find it, better, richer, and for the rest of their days."

Her lips quivered as she absorbed the story shared by the man. 'Twas a thinly veiled tale of warning if she clung to her love of Mal. That much, she kenned. Was it the truth? Och, she wasn't certain. David had married Maggie, but she'd died five years past and Fiona wasn't sure if their union happened as the man said.

Easy to find out. Brae would be more than willing to tell her.

His cup hit the table, the clatter stopping her musings. "Lass, 'tis time for you to forget the pledge of so many years ago." David captured her hand, his skin tanned and gnarled from age against hers, white and callused from hard work. He squeezed tight. "You deserve love, lass. A love of your own, no' one who is enamored by another."

Many days, she'd visit the elders' crofters and enjoyed their stories and words of wisdom. She'd tuck away bits to be savored later. Today, each word of advice grated her very last nerve. Aye, Mal was wed. Aye, he'd never seen her as his wife. 'Twas her cross to bear—the man didn't want her.

But to find another love seemed dishonest to her heart. She couldn't forget the admiration and desire she'd held for Mal within a mere thrice. And it appeared as if every clansmen she crossed wanted her to do just that. For years she pined for him, loved him, made plans for when they were wed.

Mayhap it was possible to find another to love, but she doubted it.

"Cam is a fine lad."

She rolled her eyes and huffed as she clenched a fist in frustration. "So I've been told." Too many times for her taste. Did the man ask the elders to champion his cause? Nay, surely he had more pride than that. In fact, until today's kiss, she'd never have thought of Cam having interest in her.

David sat there, grinning as if her opinion mattered not, that if enough people told her, she'd find herself miraculously in love with Cam and out of love with Mal.

"I'll visit you on the morrow," she finally said.

"Aye, Fiona." He winked and shooed her on her way. "If you see that fine Cameron, tell him good day for me."

"Grand," she muttered beneath her breath.

"Eh?"

"Aye," she said louder. Not that she'd go out of her way to find the man, though she needed to think of a way to make amends for slapping him.

She rubbed the back of her neck. 'Twas a wretched thing she'd done. And she kenned just how to fix it. She waved to Auld David and headed toward the kitchen.

"Ah, lass. To what do we owe this pleasure?" Brae looked up from kneading bread. Flour covered the table, the floor, and most of the woman's clothing.

Stifling a chuckle, Fiona said, "I need to bake something."

"Bake?" Brae asked as her voice rose in pitch. "I don't recall you ever baking before."

Aye, 'twas a problem. Yet, how hard could it be? A little flour, some honey, and mayhap some apples. She'd seen it done many a time.

"I'll be fine."

A dubious look swept over Brae's face. "Work over there," she said as she pointed toward a table to the right.

Fiona grinned and gathered what she needed. Brae kept glancing her way and shaking her head. Truly, how hard could baking be?

She mixed some flour and a wee bit of sugar, a splash of water and began pressing to try and make some type of dough. "This isn't hard," she said to herself.

She sliced some apples, tossed them in honey.

"Lass, make sure you—"

Fiona sighed and cast a look at the woman. "Brae, I ken what I'm doing." True, she mostly spent her time out of doors, but she wasn't addle minded. When she was young she'd sit and watch her mother make one sweet after another.

The woman huffed and continued to shape the bread. "Dear Lord, please protect whoever eats this tart from any malady befallin' them."

Fiona ignored Brae and her prayer. Pushing her sweaty hair from her face, she grabbed a pan and layered the dough in the bottom. Then she added the apples and just for good measure, drizzled more honey. Aye, it looked lovely.

She set it near the fire to bake.

"And just who are you baking for?" Brae asked as she moved toward her table. She sniffed at the pastry cooking on the hearth of the fire, then pulled a face.

Fiona bit at her lip, hesitant to share why she was baking. 'Twouldn't do to share the story with too many people. She wavered under Brae's direct gaze.

"Fine, I'll tell you. 'Tis for Cam."

Brae lifted her brow and crossed her arms before her amble bosom. "And what has poor Cam done to deserve your baking?"

Fiona scowled at the tease in Brae's voice. Prolonging an answer, she traced shapes with her finger in the flour spread all over the table.

"*Fiona?*"

She sighed and looked up. "He . . . I—I slapped him."

"You slapped him?" Brae yelled as her eyes widened in shock, then quickly looked about the kitchen to see if others heard her. She took a step closer to Fiona. "And why in God's gracious name would you do such a thing?" she whispered.

Fiona cast her gaze to the table. "I don't ken."

But she did. The man had kissed her. Twice. Not only that, he'd made her respond, damn him. Her body had betrayed her, the delicious heat and tremors coursing through her as quick as lightening flashed during a summer storm. Aye, stormy, 'twas an apt word to describe such swirling emotions, feelings, and desires.

All because Cam had taken liberties.

"Tell me the truth of it," Brae insisted.

She flushed and glanced at the woman. "He'd done something I didn't care for." Her voice shook. Truth be told, she'd enjoyed it, which frightened her. All these years she'd yearned for Malcolm's love . . . and Cam's kisses had her forgetting Mal was alive. Was her heart truly so fickle?

"You were vexed because he sent you food to break your fast?"

"What?"

"Aye," Brae confirmed. "The lad bade me to send food to your chamber this morn."

"Why would he do such a thing?"

"Och." Brae tossed up her hands. "Think, lass."

Fiona did, then frowned and shrugged. "Nay, I ken not."

Impossible that Cam cared for her, kiss be damned. Caught up in the moment of saving her from her fall, he'd become overly romantic. Aye, 'twas naught else. She brushed her hands on her skirt and began cleaning up her baking mess. 'Twas worth the effort to bring Cam his favorite tart.

Thoughts swirled in her head. Cam, feeling responsible? Was that why he followed her throughout the day?

Brae moved around the table with a speed that belied her age and girth. She gripped Fiona's hands within her own. "Lass, don't be a ninny. The lad is enamored with you."

Her heart pounded as she thought of Brae's words and Cam's kiss. A kiss contradicting all she held dear. She was so confused. Could she have forgotten the man she'd loved since she was a lass? And for the first man she kissed?

"Did you hear me, lass?" Brae pushed. "He's smitten."

She closed her eyes and sighed. "Brae, Cam was only helping me."

"Then why are you making the lad pastry? Everyone kens he loves sweets."

Fiona edged away, but Brae gripped her arm. "Answer me, lass."

Pulling from Brae's grasp, she crossed to the fire and checked on the pastry. 'Twas done. "I have to bring this to Cam."

"Aye. Do that, lass. And see you don't slap the lad again."

Chapter 4

She strolled toward him. *Fiona.*

Then she stopped, and started again. Carrying a platter and looking a wee bit contrite. 'Twasn't a common look for her. Bold, curious, aye. But never contrite or timid.

Cam waited.

As she glanced at him, those brilliant, green eyes filled with a shimmer of tears. His breath hitched. *God, she is beautiful.*

"I made this for you," she said briskly as she shoved the platter toward him.

He glanced down and saw a tart. Apple, apparently. Scorched around the edges; doughy and raw in the middle.

"I'm sorry, Cam."

He peered into her eyes and fell into those bottomless green depths. No matter how hard he tried to resist, he wanted naught more than to gather her in his arms and suckle on her plump lower lip. A grin lifted his mouth. She'd made him a tart. Apple was his favorite, to be sure. He eyed the treat in her hands. If it was apple, 'twas hard to discern.

He gazed at her again. The sunlight kissed her hair with a golden glow. It took all of his strength not to run his fingers through the thick tresses. Her bottom lip was set in a frown. He so wanted to skim his thumb over it, then lean in and suckle there.

The last time he had such thoughts and acted upon them, she slapped him.

Aye, *slapped* him.

He still felt the heat of her hand against his cheek. As a man—nay, a Highlander—he couldn't allow such an affront, no matter how he felt about her.

Not even if she tried to make amends.

Some of his father's words emerged from Cam's few memories of the man. *Always treat a lass as if she were the most precious thing God made. For she is.*

At this moment, it was hard to think such thoughts about Fiona.

But the memory had him holding out his hand to accept the tart. "Thank you."

Her pulse beat at the apex of her neck, fluttering beneath her pale skin as she stood before him. Despite his anger over the way she treated him, he longed to kiss the spot, touch the soft flesh he kenned would taste like flour and honey, judging by the amount of both tangled within her hair.

Instead of succumbing to his desires, he held firm.

"Please, forgive me." Her earnest tone had him taking a step forward. She palmed his forearm, her hand warm.

Blood rushed to his cods. If only she kenned how her touch affected him.

He shifted the tart and wrapped his free arm around her.

"Nay." She held up a staying hand. "Not again." Panic widened her gaze; her chest heaved.

"*Fiona.* Calm yourself."

"Don't *Fiona* me, Cam. Do not kiss me again."

Cam chuckled. "You may deny, but your eyes, lass, they say you want my kiss as much as I want to kiss you."

A soft sigh slipped past her lips, leaving them slightly open and damn, so tempting.

"I can't," she whispered. She lowered her gaze, her lashes fanned upon her flushed cheek.

He swallowed a groan.

Without another word spoken, Fiona pulled away, turned, and ran.

As Cam gazed at her, regret filled him. He was in love with a woman who clearly didn't love him.

And while he pledged she'd be his by Christmas, serious doubts filled his mind.

Fiona gripped her skirt to stop her hands from trembling. God help her, she'd wanted to kiss him. Aye, wanted to feel his strong arms around her as she snuggled against him.

How could her eye be turned by another man when Mal owned her heart from years ago as a wee lass, tagging along with the lads? Even when she'd forgotten her hoydenish ways, her devotion still belonged to the lad she'd wed in the glen behind the keep. And now it seemed disloyal, even though he was taken by another.

Och, what was she to do?

She moved to look over her shoulder then stopped herself. There could be no more interaction between them. 'Twouldn't be fair.

His gaze followed her; she felt it as she paced across the bailey. She had to get away from him, away from his scrutiny. So she entered the keep and headed toward the main hall.

"Fiona, lass," Brae called.

She resisted the urge to roll her eyes heavenward. "Aye?"

"Come and enjoy a wee bit of tea."

Not certain if she could refuse without hurting the poor woman's feelings, Fiona sat by the fire and accepted the tea.

"Drink up, lass." Brae offered a biscuit. "Did you finish looking in on the elders?"

"Nay. I've a few more to visit." Fiona dunked the biscuit into the tea and bit into the soggy, delicious mess. After she'd spoken to David and then made the tart, time had slipped by. "What do you really want to ken, Brae?"

The woman chuckled and jiggled her tea so it slipped over the rim of the cup. She hastily wiped at her apron. "I'm wondering how our Cam enjoyed the tart."

Fiona rolled her eyes heavenward. "He thanked me graciously, of course."

Brae hooted with laughter. "And after he took a bite?"

Ire flash as her face heated. "I don't ken."

"Ah, lass. I'm sure he appreciated your effort." She patted Fiona's hand.

Brae continued to nibble her tea-soaked biscuit as she glanced toward the front of the main hall. Her eyes wrinkled with concern. "You best get on with it or else 'twill be dark."

Fiona lifted her brow. "Can I finish my tea first?" Och, the woman was contrary.

At the flick of Brae's eyes, her attention on the main entrance, then back at her, Fiona swallowed a groan. For Lady Rossalyn strolled through the hall with Mairi skipping by her side.

When the lady spied her, she grinned and changed her direction so she was heading straight toward Fiona.

"Be civil, lass. 'Tis the laird's wife," Brae warned.

Och, as if she'd forgotten. The lovely woman had stolen her Mal, had taken up position at his side that should have been Fiona's. *I'd have been a fine lady of the keep.*

But, nay. Mal had brought a stranger into their clan. A woman and her child, and didn't every clansmen stop and bid the lady good day and tousle wee Mairi's dark hair. The lady herself offered gracious smiles and spoke as if she'd kenned the clan forever.

When Lady Rossalyn stood before her, Fiona glanced up briefly, then darted her gaze about to see if all were watching, catching several gapers. The nosey ones swiftly stared elsewhere.

Brae nudged her and Fiona sheepishly stood.

"Aye, m'lady?"

Lady Rossalyn reached out and grabbed her hands. "I just spent time with Auld David. Och, Fiona, the man sang your praises! Thank you for taking such good care of him."

She frowned. "Aye, 'tis my duty." No one had ever thanked her before. 'Twas a strange feeling.

The lady angled her head back and laughed. Even her laughter was graceful, blast her. "'Tis more than that. You *care* for them."

Of course she did. They were her family.

She lifted a brow at the laird's new wife. Suspicion flared and she took a stop back. Why was Lady Rossalyn being so nice? Hadn't Fiona tried to rid the keep of her?

Brae prodded her forward with her hand. "Lass," she warned with a low voice.

Fiona swallowed a sigh. "'Tis my pleasure, m'lady."

Mairi came over and clutched at her hand. Those little fingers, soft and warm, humbled her, and Fiona gave a squeeze as she looked down at the wee lass. Charming and a bit like the fairies, Mairi tilted up her chin and smiled. Pudgy cheeked and just as beautiful as her mother, the lass would have many a suiter when she was of age.

"I rode my pony."

"Ah. And did you have a grand time?" 'Twas hard to be sour with such an adorable lass.

"She's forever talking about her pony," Lady Rossalyn said with a chuckle as she slipped her arm through Fiona's.

Try as she might, Fiona couldn't pull her arm free, as the lady held tight and directed her out of the main hall, chatting the entire way. "I want you to ken, I do not blame you for what happened."

Panicked, Fiona opened her mouth to speak, but failed to find the words to apologize or even explain her actions. 'Twas a wretched thing she'd done. If her mother and father were alive to see her actions, they'd be so ashamed. Mayhap, if her mother had still been here, she'd have offered guidance with Mal, and Fiona would not have acted so rashly.

Nay, she was answerable for her own actions. And duty-bound to amend for the shame she'd brought to her family and clan.

The lady patted her hand, then kept on chattering about the upcoming holiday. "I love this time of year. Don't you, Fiona?"

She nodded, as Lady Rossalyn was already opening her mouth to speak more.

"My father wouldn't allow us to celebrate after we lost my mother. Och, 'twas a wretched time." She squeezed Fiona's arm. "And now Mairi will be old enough to enjoy the festivities."

"Aye, Mother." The lass looked to Fiona, a wide grin curling her mouth. "I'm going to eat cakes."

Fiona chuckled despite herself. The bairn was lovely, her cheeks rosy from skipping alongside, her curls rioting around her head as she bounced up and down. She'd a lot of spirit for such a wee lass.

Lady Rossalyn steered them out of the keep and into the bailey. The brisk air stung when she inhaled. Lady Rossalyn still held tight and Mairi trotted behind them, chiming in when there was talk of Christmas and the upcoming feast. The lass seemed to have an affection for sweets but even more so the promise of a present on the eve of Christmas.

Some clansmen gawked as they passed, others stood openmouthed. Fiona rolled her eyes. They'd be spreading the gossip as soon as Lady Rossalyn was out of sight. The clan did love to talk and here she was, giving them prime fodder to discuss with their neighbor. 'Twas their right, she reckoned, especially since her behavior had warranted their attention. She could only imagine what was on their minds as they observed the lady of the keep and her enemy—the woman Mal jilted—stroll through the bailey.

Lady Rossalyn leaned in close. "I'm certain we'll become dear friends." The girlish tremor of her voice, the soft tone and somewhat forlorn manner, told Fiona the lady hadn't many friends at Gordon keep. She shook her head to clear her thoughts, warring with the instinct to actually like Lady Rossalyn, when she'd vowed the woman was her staunch adversary.

The lady stiffened. "Oh, 'tis sorry I am to have bothered you." Lady Rossalyn released her and turned toward the keep.

"Wait, m'lady." Och, what had she done? Fiona reached for her, slipped her arm through hers. Held on tight when Lady Rossalyn made to pull away. She clasped Mairi's hand and brought the wee lass close.

Fiona gulped and tamped down the urge to flee. "I meant no offense. I just don't understand why you want me to be your friend after how I've treated you."

Realization must have dawned. Lady Rossalyn tilted her chin toward the men training near the stables. "Look at them. The lads don't ken the sensitive nature of a woman's heart. They play with us and expect our adoration."

Mal was putting the men through their paces and Cam was setting up another area to train. Grunts and curses filled the air. Some men landed on the ground.

Mal clapped when one man heaved another over his shoulder and the poor lad tumbled on his arse.

Cam called some of the younger lads over. Fiona gasped when he removed his shirt, then tossed it aside. 'Twasn't the first time she'd seen him without his shirt, but for some reason, reasons she didn't want to contemplate, he seemed bigger, stronger, and oh, so handsome. His body was finely hewn, as if God selected the largest oak and hand carved Cam Himself.

Each movement highlighted the bulk of his muscles. Sinew, flesh, bone. He lifted a log and hefted it upon his shoulder as if it were a sack of wheat. The sun eased over his sweat-slicked torso as he paced off an area and then tossed the log.

She tried to ignore him as he spoke to the men, pointing and demonstrating what they should do. The men signaled they understood and moved through the paces again and again. Cam guided them, cajoled them, and praised when needed. A braw leader, but he spoke with kindness and the men respected him.

"They think they can snap their fingers and we'll do their bidding." Lady Rossalyn laughed. "Little do they ken we are the ones in charge."

Fiona chuckled, but kept her eyes on the men as they began to grapple. Cam's brawn gave him the advantage. He felled one man, and then a lad came forward. Och, foolish lad. Did he ken who he was fighting? Cam was the Sargent-at-Arms because of his fighting skills. And now, as he approached the young man, each move, lunge, and parry revealed how his muscles bunched and strained. Sweat glistened in the late afternoon sun, tiny rivulets sliding down his chest. She swallowed as he bumped one of the lads on the shoulder with a fist.

"Close your mouth, Fiona."

She glanced at Lady Rossalyn and they broke into laughter.

The noised distracted the men. Cam's gaze caught hers. She grinned as the lad looked from her to Cam and sensed opportunity. With one move, Cam landed in a heap.

She laughed harder and Mairi joined in as she skipped before them.

Cam shook off the men and stood. When he spied them, he slapped his hands on his hips and glared.

"Tea, m'lady?" Fiona gestured broadly.

"'Twould be lovely, Fiona."

Chapter 5

Mal trotted over to where Cam stood, as he trained an eye on Fiona and Lady Rossalyn, making their way back to the keep. Their heads leaned close and Mairi tagged along as if she were one of the ladies and not just a wee lassie. Laughter rang through the bailey, a lovely sound, to be sure, but also unsettling.

"This doesn't bode well."

"Aye," Mal agreed.

"Just a few days ago Fiona wanted her gone." She'd put her in danger; that much, he left unspoken. Put her interest above the safety of the lady of the keep and her daughter.

Mal cocked his brow and shook his head. "Fiona is as flighty as an untamed mare."

Cam threw his head back and laughed. The description was apt, and how his fiery Fiona would balk at Mal's words. "And if she heard your assessment, you'd find yourself on your arse."

The laird slapped him on his shoulder. "She can try, lad. She can try."

Cam frowned. "You need to speak to her."

His laird dragged his fingers through his hair. "Aye. Each time I go to her chamber, I remember . . . remember the look on her face when I told her I'd married Rossalyn."

Cam remembered as well. A flash of horror, then betrayal. Her hurt had nearly killed him and he'd wanted to pull her into his arms and profess his love right there. Tell her she didn't need Mal, because she had him. Och, he was lovesick.

A lovesick cow. But she had to ken that someone loved her, would care for her, would never betray her.

"You left the keep in order to secure food stores. And you came back with a wife." He turned toward his friend, looking him directly in the eye. "'Tis no wonder she was shocked."

Mal scrubbed his hand along his jaw and stepped aside when a few grappling men nearly knocked him down. "I ken."

"For years, it was just the three of us. You had to have kenned how she felt."

"I never thought she took our vows seriously. We were so young." Mal shook his head. "She was like one of the lads."

How Cam wanted to grab Mal by the shoulders and shake some sense into the man. But he also wanted to do the same to Fiona. 'Twas a dangerous game she played and her laird had every right to bar her from the keep and demand she never return.

He prayed that wouldn't be so, because if it were, he'd follow Fiona—away from Sutherland territory, out of the Highlands—even out of Scotland. He'd hate to make the choice between his laird and the woman who owned his heart, but he'd do it in a thrice.

"I'll talk to her this eve."

Cam pledged to be there in case Mal hurt her any more, or, God forbid, she challenged him into making a rash decision. Sometimes her ire ruled her tongue. He didn't want her to say something she'd regret—or that which Mal would have to act upon.

Malcolm headed back to the men to continue training, but Cam couldn't take his eyes off Fiona as she entered the main keep with a swish to her hips and her tinkling laughter filling the air.

The sound settled deep within him, touching the heart which was already hers. He longed for her. They'd kenned each other since they were bairns. She'd held his heart from the moment Mal had beat her in a horse race and nearly crushed her spirit.

Cam had looked over his shoulder and saw the shimmer of tears in those bewitching eyes of hers when Mal had beaten her. Slowly, he had pulled up on the reins and his gelding slipped out of a gallop and into a canter. Fiona had charged past him, her body flat against her mare's neck. He remembered her whoop of victory. And when he'd reached the line of trees which had marked their finish line, he'd grinned and congratulated her.

Truly, 'twas that moment, with the wind jostling her red hair and a prideful grin curving her full mouth, he kenned he loved her.

And he'd ached for her ever since.

"M'laird," a rider—Kevin—yelled as he raced toward the men. "'Tis men about, m'laird."

"Stop." Cam grabbed the man as he tried to run by. "Tell me all."

Kevin bent over and rested his hands on his knees, trying to catch his breath. "Cam, 'tis several men past the loch." He wiped the sweat from his face. "Saw them, I did. They aren't Sutherland men."

A crowd gathered around them.

"And their tartan?" Malcolm asked as he paced through the crowd. "Was it Gordon?"

The man cursed. "Can't tell, m'laird. They wore britches."

Cam cursed, "Damn. I'll form a patrol." With any luck, they'd ferret out the men who dared to trespass on Sutherland lands.

"Be careful, Cam."

He grinned. "Always." He shouted to some of the strongest clansmen, and bade Kevin saddle up.

"God's speed," Malcolm called as they made way to leave the keep. "Send a runner if you need more help."

'Twas as always, Cam the protector and Malcolm the leader. As a team, they'd not be beat, but Gordon's brazen behavior had put them on edge. First, he tried to enter the keep and take Lady Rossalyn back. Now, he or his men could be squatting on Sutherland land. If the bastard had left clansmen behind, it could mean they plotted to attack or to cause mischief toward the Sutherlands.

From what Cam had gleaned from Mal, the contract between the clans didn't exactly assure they were at peace, only that the agreement was a harsh necessity. But the likelihood of Gordon attacking the clan in which his daughter now resided was low. And he kenned Mal wouldn't hurt Rossalyn by attacking her familial clan. So why were they still on Sutherland land?

He needed answers, his duty to the clan and their safety his only concern.

"Faster, men." He applied pressure to his gelding's sides and the animal reacted as Cam had trained him to do. They plowed through the field, rousing the fowl nesting in the long grasses.

Their horses nickered as they pushed onward, as if they felt the excitement and urgency of the situation. Kevin rode beside him, indicating the way to the site. The landscape passed by in blur.

Cam's heart pounded against his chest in anticipation of the encounter. Sweat ran down his back, dampening his shirt. How he loved an invigorating fight.

He thrived on leading, protecting his clan. 'Twas his calling.

"Up ahead, Cam."

He held up his hand to slow down the men. They dismounted and one man stayed back to secure the animals. Crouching low, staying to the tree line, they came closer, inching forward on their bellies along the ground.

Smoke scented the air along with the musty dampness of the ground and leaves.

As they caught sight of the camp, more smoke drifted upward in grayish tendrils.

No men.

"Get back to the horses."

As his clansmen ran to their mounts, Cam held back and searched the camp. No gear, food, or debris of any sort. He kicked at the smoking logs. 'Twas obvious they'd just left the camp, but were they lurking in the shadows, ready to launch an attack?

"Cam," Kevin whispered. "No sight of them."

Was it that simple? Had they left to go back to Gordon territory? Cam set his hands at his waist and looked about the area. There had to be a signal, some indication of who they were and where they'd taken cover.

"We'll hide the horses and camp here tonight." He looked toward the trees, trying for a sense of any danger lurking in their dark depths. "Send a rider back to the keep and let Laird Sutherland ken we'll remain on patrol."

"Aye, Cam."

The horses were secured in a glen away from the camp. Cam instructed the men to surround the chosen area but remain hidden until they heard his telltale whistle which indicated attack.

He found his own spot, high upon a crag. The height and distance allowed for a clear view of the camp and the surrounding areas. He leaned against the rock and ignored the rumble of his stomach. Och, in their haste they hadn't secured provisions. And now, with their alert on high, to strike a fire could alert the strangers of their presence.

The last thing he'd eaten was Fiona's tart. Or what resembled a tart. 'Twas possibly the worst thing he'd eaten, with overly sweet apples and burnt crust. But the pride shining in her eyes as she handed it to him forced him to at least try the tart, and since he kenned gossip ran swiftly through the clan, he finished it lest word otherwise might reach dear Fiona.

Och, her gesture was kind and he kenned she wished to apologize for her earlier behavior. He would have accepted a kiss, truth be told. 'Twould have been more appropriate considering she'd struck him. But Fiona had refused his kiss.

If she were here now, as the sun dipped beneath the trees, he'd thank her for the tart and let her ken he forgave her. He rubbed his face where she'd hit him. Aye, it had smarted. He leaned against the craggy rock at his back. Darkness settled around him, and soon it would cloak his location. His stomach growled again and he wished Fiona's tart had been bigger.

"Cam."

Was his imagination tricking him? Had his wish to see her made her appear?

"Cam?"

He groaned. She'd followed them.

Clouds shifted and the moonlight did little to hide her form as she scrambled up on the rock and handed him a cloth bag. "I brought the other men their food first." She nodded toward the camp. "'Tis the perfect place to hide."

"Really." The single word held a heavy dose of sarcasm. "You found me."

She waved at him. "The men told me where you were."

He opened the bag and sighed with pleasure. Mutton and bread. "No tart?"

Her chuckle drew a smile on his own face. Och, what a sensual laugh she had. It drove desire straight to his cods.

"'Twas wretched, I ken." She settled in beside him and began pulling the bread apart.

Her presence, the heat of her body, just the fact she was the woman he loved, made his blood roar. Oh, how he wanted to pull her into his arms and kiss her senseless, until she was full of desire and mayhap he'd be able to complete his dreams of seduction. With a quick glance he eyed her, gauging her mood.

The light of the moon eased over her smooth skin, haloing her like an angel. Golden streams of light slipped along her jaw, her long neck, over her chest and into the gap of her *liene*. How he envied the moon and the intimacy of its touch along her skin.

"Have you seen any men?"

"Nay," he croaked.

Fiona turned to him and laid her hand on his arm. Her brows quirked upward. "Are you well?"

He jerked back from her incendiary touch. "I'm fine."

She immediately stiffened.

"Fiona—"

"I'll be leaving." She stood and moved to climb down the crag. She squared her shoulders and lifted up her chin. "Apparently, you do not forgive me."

Bollocks, he would not feel badly for worrying about her. "You should have never come. 'Tis too dangerous."

She wagged her finger at him. "I ken. But I was worried about the men missing their evening meal and Lady Rossalyn suggested I bring supplies."

Dear God. "Lady Rossalyn? Did Mal ken what she suggested?"

Even in the dark of the eve, he saw her flush. "We didn't have time to speak with Mal."

He lifted up her chin. "Fiona, 'twas foolish to travel on your own when you ken we are looking for strange men."

She moved out of his reach. "I am not an *eejit*. I rode with Kevin. He had to report to Mal and I traveled back with him." She laced her arms before her chest. "And he appreciated my efforts."

He was going to kill the man. Truly kill him. Cam's blood chilled at the thought of Fiona riding through dangerous territory. Kevin be damned. He was only one man and the size of the camp indicated several more than that. "You shouldn't be here and if Mal kenned, you'd feel his fury."

"Ha," she retorted with a nervous laugh. "I've handled the both of you since we were bairns."

What was he to do with this spirited woman? "Truly?" Handled them? Ire spiked and he was close to leaving her here and heading back to the keep.

She squared her shoulders. "Aye. You ken I can take care of myself. I've bested you many a time. Don't you remember, or does your manly arrogance force you to forget?"

"Indeed," he drawled.

She had the audacity to laugh. "Do you not remember all of those times I sped past you? Or when I caught more fish than you?"

He'd had enough of her smugness. "I let you win," he growled as he inched forward, so close her hot breath moistened his skin. "And I didn't bait my hook."

Fiona's eyes widened, then she jerked back as if *he'd* slapped her. "Why would you do such a thing?"

Frustrated, he clenched a fist in his hair. Och, why had he spoken what he and Mal pledged not to? His thoughts warred with his heart that had ached with desire for so long. It had nearly torn him apart witnessing her tag after Malcolm.

Month after month. Year after year. She'd follow their laird. For such a feisty woman, she turned into a simpering fool around Mal. She'd coo, pout, or hang on to his every word. 'Twas a wretched display of lovesickness.

"Why, Cam?" she repeated, jarring him out of his memories.

She'd never leave him alone if he didn't tell her, he knew that about her. After a sigh, he said, "Because . . . because I love you. Always have."

She gasped and covered her mouth with her hand. Then anger sparked in her eyes. She punched his arm. "Don't be daft. You don't love me."

He raised her chin, rubbed his thumb along her plump, lower lip. "I do, Fiona. I love your spirit. The way your nose scrunches when you are thinking." He smoothed the hair from her face. "I love you."

"You can't. You don't." Panic widened her eyes. She pulled from him. "I—I have to go."

His fingers slipped against the material of her *liene* as he reached for her. "Wait." He'd been too bold. He should have waited for a better time. He pinched the bridge of his nose and exhaled harshly. "I didn't mean to—"

"Nay." As her gaze met his, coldness filled them. "You do not love me."

He chuckled at her vehemence. "Aye, I do."

She shook her head. "No matter. I do not love you, Cam. I never will."

His world crashed around his shoulders as dread filled him; dread and regret for speaking so rashly about his feelings.

She scrambled down with such speed, for a moment he thought he'd dreamt her presence on the crag. Yet her words were anything but a dream.

I do not love you, Cam. I never will.

Fiona pushed her mare as fast as she could in the evening light. Her heart lodged in her throat. Why had Cam professed his love? Tears pooled in her eyes as frustration and anger filled her. Och, she was confused.

The keep rose before her and she rode to the palisade and hopped off her mare. After wiping her face free of tears, she entered and strode toward the stables.

"Fiona!"

Lady Rossalyn raced toward her. Concern creased her face. "Why have you returned?"

"Cam said he loved me." Once again tears brimmed her eyes. Why did he have to say he loved her? Didn't he realize it changed everything? From this point forward, their relationship would be different. She'd have to avoid him and he, being the man he was, would be kind, but she'd always sense his longing. And feel guilty about it.

Did he think she'd forgotten her love for Malcolm just because he'd wed? Did he think if he told her he loved her, she'd fall into his arms and return his sentiments? Aye, she'd kissed him. And enjoyed it, truth be told. But her heart couldn't be swayed so quickly.

Lady Rossalyn pulled her into a hug. "That wretched man. How dare he tell you something so nice." Humor laced her voice.

Fiona chuckled and cried at the same time. "You do not ken and I fear I can't tell you."

The lady patted her on the back and said, "Fiona, you can tell me anything."

Strange how this woman, whom she first thought of as a foe, was slowly becoming her confidant. Still, the words wouldn't form. For how was she to tell the laird's gentle lady the reason she loathed Cam's words was because her heart belonged to Mal?

Certainly, Mal had spoken to Rossalyn of Fiona's affection, but 'twas a different situation for Fiona to actually say the words as well. Such a confession of her heart would surely make Lady Rossalyn hate her.

"Come, Fiona. I'll wet some tea and we'll have ourselves a chat." She gripped Fiona's elbow and guided her toward the keep. "We'll have privacy in my chambers."

She jerked to a stop. Lady Rossalyn's chamber? In truth, 'twas Laird and Lady Sutherland's chamber. How could she be in the very room where Mal and Rossalyn slept?

"Dear God Almighty, lass! Mal is with his men awaiting Cam's return. He'll not disturb us." With that said, Lady Rossalyn turn on her heel and headed toward the Laird's chamber.

Fiona rubbed the back of her neck and stood for a moment as she contemplated which path to take. Follow the lady and enjoy a cup of tea? Or to her own chamber to wallow in her misbegotten misery? The tea won out. She'd not only quench her thirst but also continue to forge a friendship. A friendship she sorely needed.

'Twasn't often the women of the clan included her. Despite Mal's claim 'twas her beauty which kept the other lasses from befriending her, Fiona kenned she was often grumpy and brisk. Who could blame the others for not liking her? But something deep down pushed her to find a friend. With her parents gone and Mal now married, and Cam . . . och, she didn't ken how things sat with Cam.

Fiona was running out of options. And truth be told, if she'd become familiar with Lady Rossalyn sooner, she'd never have tried to force her to leave the clan.

The beautiful lady of the keep had surprised her in many ways. Mostly, her forgiveness of Fiona's heinous actions spoke of her character. But she was strong and had settled into the clan as if born to it. People seemed to adore her and wee Mairi. Aye, 'twas fitting for Rossalyn to be the lady of the keep.

"Sit, Fiona," Lady Rossalyn said as Fiona entered the laird's chamber.

'Twasn't the first time she'd been in the chamber. Many a time Malcolm's mother would summon them and give a stern reprimand for their pranks. But then it was Mal's parents' room, filled with their clothing, Laird Sutherland's weapons, and the lavender scent which seemed to always linger on Mal's mother. Fiona glanced about as if sensing the ghost of the former laird and lady. Their presence had lessened and Lady Rossalyn was making her mark on the chamber.

Fiona sat and fiddled with a napkin, her nerves a bit rattled from the day's events and the memories the chamber wrought.

Despite her unease, she slowly began to relax as the warmth of the crackling fire heated her surroundings.

"Start from the beginning." Lady Rossalyn lifted her brow as she spoke and gave a look that brooked no room for refusal.

With a heavy sigh, she told the sad tale. As the words left her mouth and filled the room, Fiona's nerves tangled once again as she comprehended what a fool she was. "You see? He has changed everything."

"For the better, I feel." Lady Rossalyn placed her hands over hers and squeezed. "He's a fine man, honorable, the best of Malcolm's men."

Guilt ate at her. All of what the lady said was true, indeed Cam was one of their best. But he wasn't the man she'd spent her nights dreaming about and her days following around trying to gain his attention at all costs.

Fiona rose and moved to the fireplace. She held her shaking hands toward the heat.

"I ken how you feel about Malcolm. He explained all after Mairi and I were rescued."

The scrape of a chair against the stone flooring alerted Fiona that Lady Rossalyn was moving toward her.

"I'm sorry Mairi and I have upset your plans . . . your dreams." She touched Fiona's shoulder. "But—"

Och, the woman was truly gracious. Beautiful and gracious, surely she deserved Mal more than Fiona. "Nay. No need to speak the truth. Malcolm does not love me as I loved him." Love or loved, now her emotions hovered in between and sometimes leaned toward one emotion, then the other at any given moment.

She covered her face with her hands. Blast it, 'twas confusing.

"He loves you," Rossalyn said, her soft tone motherly. "He's not in love with you." The last words were a whisper and Fiona appreciated how gently she relayed the truth of the situation. A truth which was clear and had been clear from the moment Fiona had rode to greet Mal and his men and saw the lovely Lady Rossalyn.

Emotion choked any response. Fiona merely shrugged and continued to stare at the fire. The orange and red flames blurred through her tears. Lady Rossalyn turned and left the chamber.

As the door clicked shut, all Fiona could think was why the truth needed to hurt so much.

Chapter 6

The holiday was nearly upon them and there was no news as to the men who'd camped on Sutherland soil. They never returned to their spot in the woods and no other clues were found to determine their business. Cam and his men continued to patrol the area and follow any trails which weren't created by the Sutherland clan. Yet, persistent squalls of snow rendered many of their efforts fruitless.

They rode off once again as the early morning mist and snow swirled about the hooves of the steeds. Fiona kept watch from her chamber. A chill raced up her spine and she rubbed her arms to ward it off.

"Such nonsense," she said to herself. Her worries were baseless. Cam and his men were braw and well trained. Cam wouldn't have it any other way. No doubt they'd dispatch any threat without an issue.

Yet . . . fear still jangled her nerves. She grabbed her *arisaid* and headed to the bailey. Wrapping the woolen material tight around her, she kept warm as she strode to the palisade. Men protected the gate and stood before her as she attempted to step outside the keep's wall.

"No one is to pass."

She slapped her hands on her hips and the wind whipped her *arisaid* against her legs. "I'll just be outside the wall."

"Nay, Fiona. I'll not disobey Cam's orders."

Cam.

Of course he'd try to keep her inside the keep. She seethed as she turned on her heel and stomped back to the main hall. Mayhap Lady Rossalyn would like a bit of fresh air. Surely, Cam's orders didn't include her as well.

The man seemed to want to vex her at every turn. They'd yet to speak since their discussion in the woods. His words haunting her, she worried for her battered heart and even a bit for Cam's heart. He professed to have loved her since he could remember. How could she not have seen it? 'Twasn't as if he'd mooned over her. In fact, there were certain times she had suspected Cam didn't care for her and found her a nuisance.

He'd drag Malcolm away to train with swords or arrows, even when the man knew she couldn't participate. And in the evenings when they gathered after a meal, Cam and Mal would sit with the rest of the lads and make it apparent they didn't want her presence.

"Stop vexing us," Cam would mutter. "Go sit with the lasses."

But she didn't. Instead, she'd go to her chamber and plot how to gain Mal's attention.

And now, now Cam claimed he'd always loved her.

Fiona's heart clenched as she remembered the look of admiration on his face. 'Twas as if saying the words had set him free of every secret he'd held against his will. Such a braw man, confessing something so dear.

And when she'd fled, when she said she didn't love him, the enchanting smile had vanished and she feared . . . feared she'd hurt him beyond measure.

She chewed on her lip, trying to think of something other than the shock on Cam's face.

The shock and hurt.

She pulled up short and covered her mouth. 'Twas the same shock and hurt she'd felt when Malcolm had announced his marriage.

How could she make it better? She feared there was no way.

Brae waved at her. "Fiona, come and aid with the shortbread."

Frowning, unwilling to spend time with anyone, still Fiona crossed to the table where many lasses were mixing the flour and butter. Shortbread was a clan favorite.

The lasses chattered as they worked and gossiped about the upcoming dance, taking place on Christmas Eve. And many giggled about which lad they'd pin their sights on.

"You're a quiet one, our Fiona. No lad on your mind?"

She glared at Brae who kenned the direction of her heart. Her throat scratched as she tried to think of a witty retort. All that came to mind was the woman had the right of it, she needed to think of something else and forget her affection for Malcolm.

"Shortbread!" Lady Rossalyn exclaimed as she came to the table. "'Tis our laird's favorite."

Without thinking, Fiona rolled her eyes heavenward, earning a swift kick from Brae. She leaned down and rubbed her shin, thinking the lady had learned her husband's likings very quickly.

Lady Rossalyn chatted and even rolled some dough. Fiona tried to ignore her, but found it impossible not to allow a small grin at her energetic spirit. She already kenned everyone's name and relationships. As much as Fiona loathed to admit it, she truly liked her.

Then Lady Rossalyn came to her side and asked, "Fiona, would you mind helping me with Mairi?"

She furrowed her brow. "Aye." How could she possibly help? She worked with the elders of the clan. The children seemed to be leery of her and she was equally uneasy around them. When bairns were born, she'd *ohh* and *ahh*, but always fearful to hold their wee, squirming bodies. What if they cried? What if she dropped them? Yet, even with her uncertainty, Fiona longed for her own bairn and kenned her fears would melt away when she held a babe borne of her body.

Lady Rossalyn immediately laced her arm through Fiona's. "'Tis no help needed, but I wanted to finish our conversation."

Och, 'twas the last conversation she wanted to have, discussing the man she loved with his wife.

Once again they headed toward the laird's chamber.

"Tea is being sent and then we shall not be disturbed."

As they entered the laird's chamber, Malcolm was securing his tartan with a leather belt.

"Ah, m'ladies."

Fiona looked everywhere except at Malcolm, suddenly shy and uncomfortable, when she usually tossed barbs or witty remarks at him.

Lady Rossalyn released her arm and strolled to her husband. She stood on tiptoe and kissed him. He grinned and cupped her cheek, the action so intimate, Fiona felt like an intruder and shifted her gaze. Mostly, her heart pinged with loneliness.

"I'm joining Cam today."

"Take care, my husband." Lady Rossalyn kissed him again and he nodded at Fiona as he left the chamber.

He paused in the doorway. His gaze met hers. Momentary regret seemed to fill them. "Anything you'd like me to say to Cam?"

"Nay," she replied. She had nothing to say to the man. At least nothing she'd tell Malcolm. Her next conversation with Cam would be in private and she hoped she'd be able to explain her feelings without damaging his any further.

Mal sighed. "Rossalyn, love. Can I speak with Fiona alone?"

Lady Rossalyn glanced her way, then said, "Aye." She squeezed Fiona's arm as she walked by.

Fiona reached for her, sent her a pleading look to remain in the chamber. How was she going to face him alone? What could she say? There were no words that would allow her to fully express her regret.

Lady Rossalyn shook her head. "I'll be right outside." She exited the chamber and shut the door.

Fiona took a step as if to follow. Mal cleared his throat and she froze.

"I want to apologize to you," he said.

She swung to face him. Had she heard him correctly? "Nay, Mal. 'Tis me who should beg your forgiveness. What I have done 'twas shameful. Horrible." Tears filled her eyes and her stomach clenched when she recalled her actions.

He came forward. "Look at me, Fiona."

She peered up at him. Stared at his handsome face. Those eyes of his—och, the tiny scar near his right brow. He'd fallen into the loch and skimmed his head on a rock. She swallowed a sigh.

He gripped her hands within his large ones. "I love Rossalyn." The way he spoke, so sincere and heartfelt, it was obvious he adored his new wife.

Sharp pain pierced her heart. "Aye, she's lovely."

His soft chuckle eased around her. "She is. And so are you. You've been a dear friend for many years. I want you to ken I treasured our friendship."

She shrugged, not certain what to say. The air in the room seemed to disappear and she had trouble breathing. Here Malcolm stood, professing his love of another woman. The keep didn't crumble down around her. 'Twas odd, truth be told. It hurt, but not as badly as she'd thought.

"I was wretched toward Lady Rossalyn and Mairi."

His gaze turned grim. "They could have been hurt, Fiona." He released her hands, then swept his through his hair. "What if they'd died?"

Tears raced down her cheeks. "I ken. I—I just didn't think." She wiped her nose with the back of her hand. She'd always been a messy crier.

"You are impulsive and quick to anger. You put my wife in danger." He crossed his arms before his chest. "What do you propose I do?"

He was asking her? Surprised, she sat in the chair before the fire. "I don't ken."

"There has to be a decision and I'd rather you and I determine one."

'Twas better, she agreed. But what would be the best choice? Surely, Mal wouldn't punish her with a whip? "I could work in the kitchen."

Mal gave a bark of laughter. "That would be punishment for the rest of us."

She laughed along with him, then sobered. "I don't ken what we could do."

"I'll think of something. I promise you, it won't be too harsh."

He was being magnanimous. "How can you not throw me into the dungeon?"

"Och, Fiona. I'd never do that to you." He peered down at her. "But this is serious. You ken?"

She did. 'Twas the worst thing she'd ever done. "I'm so sorry, Mal. I . . . I just don't ken why I did it." Aye, she did. She was jealous and mean. Mad at Mal and the rest of the people in the keep, but especially Lady Rossalyn.

After wiping the tears from her face, she stood and walked over to him. "I promise I will not bring harm to Lady Rossalyn or Mairi. I promise on my life."

Mal pulled her into a hug and kissed the top of her head as one would a sister. He loved her but wasn't in love with her. Wasn't that what Rossalyn had said? She was the pesky sister trailing after him and Cam. A sigh shuddered from her.

Malcolm released her, held her at arm's length. "We will find a solution."

She offered a wavering smile. "Aye."

"May I enter?"

They turned to the threshold. Lady Rossalyn peeked around the door with a hopeful gleam in her eyes.

"Aye," Mal said as he held Fiona's gaze. He gave an encouraging jerk of his chin.

"Grand." She swept into the room as if nothing untoward had happened. As if Fiona hadn't tried to get rid of her and her sweet daughter. "Malcolm," she began with a pinched brow, "why is Fiona crying?"

Mal looked to heaven as if praying for strength. "I didn't beat her, wife."

Fiona stepped forward and rested her hand on Mal's arm. "Truly, Lady Rossalyn. M'laird was nothing but kind."

"M'laird," she said with a snort. "Seems to be a brute, leaving a woman in tears."

"Truly, he was good to me." She must make the lady ken just how wonderful Malcolm was being. The man could have had her whipped or sent to the dungeons. And here he was, showing infinite kindness and love.

If she weren't already in love with him—she'd fall in love with him.

"See, I was nothing but a gentleman."

"Leave us." Lady Rossalyn's voice chimed musically. "We've much to discuss."

Mal kissed his wife on the cheek. "I've to see to Cam." With a quick salute in Fiona's direction, he left the chamber.

"I'm glad you had a chat. Now you can forget what happened and we can move forward." She looked pointedly at Fiona. "'Tis what Mal wants. What I want."

There was nothing the lady could say that would make Fiona feel better. Right then, she pledged to strive to make up for her actions for as long as it took.

A serving lass brought tea and they sat before the window for a few silent minutes.

"Lady Rossalyn," she said to break the silence. "'Tis nothing more to discuss."

"Call me Rossalyn."

Och, and Mal would have her head.

"Firstly, I don't want you to discount Cam's proclamation of love. He is a grand man and you'd do well together."

Before any words of protest even left Fiona's mouth, Lady Rossalyn—*nay, Rossalyn*—shook her head firmly to stop her from speaking. Then reached out and clasped Fiona's hands.

The lady of the keep had a stronger grip than Fiona had originally thought. Strong enough to be lady of the keep, for when Fiona tried to pull away, Rossalyn held tight.

"Tell me," she began, "why do you think you're in love with Malcolm?"

Why ask such a question? Fiona's stomach roiled. Searching her mind for an answer, she pulled her hand from Rossalyn's tight grasp. Burying her face in her tea seemed to create a decent excuse not to speak. There were so many reasons, but none she could verbalize. To say the least, it would make Rossalyn uncomfortable.

"Ah-ha!" Rossalyn clapped her hands. "See, you are not in love with Malcolm."

Fiona's cheeks heated as her teacup clattered on the saucer. Her brow furrowed as she thought about the reasons she loved Mal.

"Fiona, you can't even give me one reason why you love him."

Springing from the chair, nearly knocking it backward, Fiona paced the chamber that used to be familiar to her. An extra tartan now draped across a chair. Mairi's toys littered the floor before the hearth. Rossalyn's chemise was folded neatly atop the chest of drawers.

'Twas a family chamber, each contributing a bit of themselves so they could live happily together.

For so long, she'd deemed this should be her chamber. Yet she couldn't think of a compelling reason why she loved Malcolm. Aye, he was strong. But so was every other Highlander. They'd played and fought and enjoyed their youth. He'd been a loyal friend.

In the past her heartbeat had nearly burst from her chest when he was near. Today, when she'd stood watching him fasten his tartan as he spoke with her, then after he hugged her and kissed her head, there was—

Nothing.

Not even a shimmer in her heart.

Her eyes grew wide as she spun toward Lady Rossalyn. "Mayhap, you are right."

The lady squealed, joining her in the middle of the chamber. "Now tell me, when you think of Cam, what does your heart say?"

Fiona blinked and frowned. "He's kind, gentle—"

Kind. Gentle.

She covered her mouth with her hand. Nay, she wasn't in love with Cam.

Lady Rossalyn cast her a speculative glance, crossed her arms over her chest; tapped her foot. "Truly, you are the most frustrating woman I have ever met." She grasped Fiona's elbows lightly. "Aye, frustrating."

With a wry smile, Fiona sighed, "So I've been told. Many times."

"Can't you see? You love the man." She shook Fiona lightly. "It's as plain as can be."

Fiona twisted away and pinched the bridge of her nose. Confusion settled around her and she pressed her lips together to keep from agreeing. *'Tis impossible.*

"I do *not* love Cam."

With that said, she left the chamber and a chuckling Lady Rossalyn whose parting words floated out the doorway.

"We'll see, Fiona. We'll see."

Cam kept watch as Laird Sutherland and more men galloped toward him. His men craved relief and glad he was to see their laird anticipated those needs. He grinned as Mal and one of the other clansmen seemed to be racing. Always a competitive man, Mal had the edge by a horse-length.

When Mal reached his side, he quickly dismounted and handed the reins over to one of the men. His chest heaved and he slapped his horse on the rear.

"Cool him down," he instructed Kevin.

Cam lifted his brow. "He's barely winded."

Mal flashed a grin. "Aye, 'tis the best stallion in the stable."

'Twas the truth of it. Mal's stable boasted many fine steeds. And as laird, Mal rode the strongest of the herd.

"I've brought more men. And news."

Instinct took over. "News?"

Mal cuffed him on the back. "No need to look so worried, but when I left the keep, Fiona and m'lady were having tea in my chamber."

Dear God, what were the women planning? "I warned you."

"You did." Mal heaved a sigh. "I spoke with Fiona."

Cam slid a glance at his laird. "Aye?"

"We've come to an agreement to forgive. But I've to come up with a punishment."

What a position to be in. Having to determine the punishment for a friend was difficult to say the least. "*Bollocks.* What will you do?"

Mal grunted. "I do not ken."

"Mayhap, they are discussing what you should do as we speak." Cam grinned at the sudden frown that darkened Mal's face.

"I'll question Rossalyn later to see what transpired."

Cam threw back his head and laughed. "Question your wife?"

Mal grimaced, then dragged his fingers through his hair. "I've my ways. Tell me, have you seen any of Gordon's men?"

With a quick shake of his head, Cam pivoted about on a boot heel, and inspected the surrounding forest. Call it instinct, training, or luck; he kenned they were being observed. But after searching every area, they'd yet to find the men or clues as to who they were. In his bones he felt these were Gordon clansmen, roaming where they did not belong.

And no matter how much he tried to focus and strategize, Fiona's enchanting smile interrupted his thoughts.

Regardless of her reaction when he proclaimed his love, he was confident she'd come to see his way of thinking. Mayhap 'twas what she and Lady Rossalyn were speaking about.

"Keep relief men coming and we'll wait them out," he finally replied.

Malcolm gave him an appraising look. "I've no doubt you will."

"Has Gordon made an attempt to visit Lady Rossalyn again?" The man was trouble, which both he and Mal kenned the first moment they met him. But the unforgiving terrain had forced Malcolm's hand, especially after his father's death.

The old laird had forged tenuous alliances, alliances that had faltered upon his death. Nothing Mal did convinced the neighboring clans into continuing the agreements. Sometimes, Cam wondered if Gordon had forced the other clans to refuse them. 'Twas too convenient, and when Gordon approached Mal with the proposed agreement, Mal had no choice but to agree.

Lady Rossalyn hadn't talked of her father, except to apologize to the clan for his treachery. She'd spoken so eloquently, some of the women had tears in their eyes. Her profession of love for their laird, coupled with Mairi's determined stance at her mother's side, had the clan eagerly pledging their support and clamoring to get closer to their new lady of the keep. As for the details of Clan Gordon business, Rossalyn had been kept out of it.

Cam's main task was to keep the clan safe, and ensure nothing happened to his laird and lady. No more focusing on Fiona, for his feelings interfered with his duty.

Bollocks, how could he stop thinking of her? His blood heated at the memory of her kisses, the feel of her curves beneath his hand and the fire, ah, the fire of her gaze. When she warred with herself during and after their kiss, such a tumult of emotions had flittered through her eyes. Shock, ire, and aye, fury aimed at him. Why she fought the attraction was beyond him—

Nay, I ken why.

Her childhood infatuation with Mal.

Cam glanced at his laird, now relaying instructions to the other men. In finding love with Lady Rossalyn, Malcolm probably didn't realize how pained Fiona was by his actions. Mayhap none of them realized how deeply Fiona hurt.

But would a woman, who responded to his kisses as Fiona had done, still hold feelings for another man? Her lips had driven him mad. At times he still felt the imprint of her curvaceous body against his. Full breasts, those long limbs and the apex of her thighs where she cradled his cock as their hips met . . .

Blood seared a path through his body. God, how he wanted her. Needed her.

"Cameron?"

He turned toward Mal. "Aye?"

Concern flickered in his laird's eyes. "Would you like to return to the keep?"

For an instant, Cam entertained returning. But his duty to the clan overrode his desire to see Fiona. Since their last words spoken were in anger, mayhap some time to think on other things would help them both. Truth be told, he'd been avoiding her each time he'd returned to the keep, giving her time, and trying not to pressure her.

"Nay," he retorted.

"Grand. Send word if you find the bastards." He slipped his sword from its sheath and swung it in an arch. "I'd like a chance to dispatch them to hell."

Cam chuckled. When Mal was angered, 'twas as if he turned into a demon bent on vengeance. And if Gordon had tried to hurt the woman he loved, Cam would wear just as fierce of a scowl on his face.

"Supplies will be brought again in the morn," Mal said.

They clasped hands and gave curt nods.

Silently, Laird Sutherland mounted his horse and whistled to the men. With a quick command they eased their horses into a gallop. Hoof beats sounded like thunder as thick clouds of snow and dirt floated about the men.

Casting an eye over his steed, Cam nearly ordered him to be readied for the ride back to camp.

Duty. He had a duty to his clan.

He'd have to wait until his dreams to see her.

See the woman he loved.

Chapter 7

In the solitude of her chamber, Fiona sighed and rubbed the back of her neck. When would Christmas be over? Baking, cleaning, and festooning the hall with holly and mistletoe was wearing on her every last nerve.

Her gaze lit on her bed and she noticed an *arisaid* was folded neatly in the center with a small slip of parchment on top. She frowned and leaned down to pick up the parchment, then snapped her hand back and glanced about the room to see if anything else was amiss.

With a sigh, she picked up the parchment once again.

To keep you warm, Yours, Cam

After rereading the note three times, she dropped it on her bed and stared at the new *arisaid*. Why had he done this? When had he done this?

Creating an *arisaid* took time. Cam had been on patrol for the past few days. And how did he find out she'd torn hers? A rent could be easily mended if she took the time to do so.

Fiona crossed her arms over her chest and looked at the offending garment.

He would have had to ask the weaver to make it before the evening in the woods. Before he proclaimed his love for her and before she'd told him she didn't love him.

Slumping down on the bed, she fingered the woolen material. Beautiful, soft, and she kenned warmer than her old *arisaid*. The tartan showed the pride of the Sutherland Clan, bold colors of deep green and vibrant blue woven together with precision.

Guilt nudged at her as she unfolded the garment and slipped it over her shoulders. She snuggled in.

A tear slipped over her lashes and trickled down her cheek. What an *eejit* she was. Crying over the simple gift of an *arisaid*. But her heart was touched by such thoughtfulness. With such an offering, Cam had shown a desire for taking care of her.

When was the last time someone did something so generous for her? She loved caring for others, especially the elders, but there were times when she longed for someone to treat her similarly. It wasn't as if she were looking to be pampered. Nay, hard work was all she'd known. In truth, she wouldn't ken what to do if she weren't busy.

But the lass side of her, the one who liked the pretty wildflowers growing in the glen or sipping tea before a fire and listening to a tale spun by an admirer, sometimes needed those sweet moments to remind her she was a woman.

And in her mind, the only person she'd ever seen herself sitting before the hearth with was Malcolm.

He'd been one of the steady people in her life. When her parents had died, Mal was there to console her. If there were fish to be caught, Mal would seek her out. And where there was time to play, Mal would challenge her to a horse race.

Mal and *Cam*. She sniffed and tugged the *arisaid* tighter about her shoulders. Another steady presence. The vexingly handsome, quick-witted Cam, with his infectious laughter. 'Twas hard to think of a moment when the three of them weren't together.

Something had been in his eyes, that moment when he said he loved her. Such absolute faith in what he was saying. He wasn't embarrassed or arrogant as some men were wont to be. His pride didn't dictate his words, those words spoken with passion and deep emotion. He'd said he loved her with such joy and raw honesty, she'd been taken aback.

Frightened.

And then she'd tried to hurt him, dissuade him of any romantic notions. To protect herself for risking her heart to another.

She cried out and clutched her chest.

I've been a fool.

Leaves rustled. Shadows moved between the trees.

An arrow whistled past Cam's ear as a battle cry filled with early evening air.

"To arms!" he called as he reached for his sword and slipped his dirk from its sheath tied onto his calf. He gripped the hilt of his sword and aimed it toward the men emerging from the woods as if they were forged from the trees.

Eerie forms slipping from the forest and moving through the moonless night, the darkness hid their faces until they were a few paces away.

Chaos rained upon their camp as a steady stream of men rushed in.

"Timothy, your left," Cam yelled through the din. He slashed at a man. Then stabbed another.

Lifting his sword, he stuck the young lad who'd nearly pierced his flesh. "Ian, behind you!"

Swords clanked. Men grunted. Shouted. Commanded.

Mist and blood slicked the ground as Cam grappled with another of the intruders. His muscled strained. How many men were there? Toppling one, he attacked another.

With each man, he tried to see if he kenned them from Gordon keep. None seemed familiar.

Bollocks. More came at them. Were they spawning from the devil?

His men fought, and their training paid off. Each drill, contest, and test of strength and will was put to use at this very moment.

The stench of blood filled the air as men fell. Some of them his own, blast it. The situation needed to be controlled.

He lifted his arm and gave a silent command. Several of his men sidled past their foe and circled around.

"Hold," Cam yelled until his men were in position. As he waited for a few of his men to assume their stances, he fought the latest aggressor before him.

A dirk dragged across his forearm. "You bastard." Cam struck back with a cut of his own, then with the hilt of his sword he punched the man in the face.

Down he fell.

A quick survey of the others, and he shouted, "Strike!"

His men converged on the enemy. Moments passed as if shifting through time at a slow pace. Grunts and screams of defeat filled the air.

"Cam, watch out."

He turned, lifting his sword as he did so. Steel hit steel. The force vibrated down his arm. The adversary lifted his sword and with a sneer on his ugly face, struck again.

Cam pushed up and took a step closer. Swords locked at the hilt. The foul breath of the man brushed against his face. With all of his strength, he shoved, trying to back him into defeat.

"You will die, Sutherland," the cretin growled.

"After you," Cam ground out, every muscle straining as he met the enemy's strength.

The sounds around them faded. Fog filled the air, trailed the ground. 'Twas as if he and this solo foe fought alone and not in the middle of a skirmish. The man glanced to the right.

"*Cam.*"

Sharp pain filled his side; made him bellow and arch away from his opponent. Another offender had dragged his dirk along Cam's ribs. The gleam of satisfaction on his sneering face conveyed he planned to finish Cam off.

Daniel ran to his side, calling to Allan for help.

They quickly dispatched both men to hell.

With ragged breaths, Cam stood staring at the carnage as the surviving bastards fled. Three of his men were down, but luckily still alive.

"See if you can determine who they are," he instructed Timothy. "Get the injured men back to the keep. Flank them on each side."

His man nodded, then directed others to gather the injured men.

Cam winced as he gingerly touched his side. When he lifted his hand it was covered in blood.

"You need to get back to the keep." Allan studied the slice in Cam's side.

'Twas a wee scratch. "In time. I have to see to the men."

Allan grunted. "Aye." He started gathering any weapons left behind. "No markings."

Damn. But it mattered not. They kenned whom the men represented. There was no other option. By God, if he ever saw Gordon again he'd rip him limb by limb. The man had threatened them one too many times. Next time he encroached on Sutherland Keep, he'd find himself dead.

Once Mal learned of the treachery, Gordon would have the both of them after him. God would not have mercy on their rotten souls. And if necessary, he'd track them to the hellhole they emerged from.

He gathered all he could from the camp and moved to mount his horse. Pain seared his side and a rush of blood oozed down his tartan. He hissed as he urged his horse forward. Once they were clear of the trees, the animal slipped into a full gallop.

Cam pulled back on the reins and his mount reared up. *Bollocks*. He grimaced and shifted a hand to his side. His vision blurred as the keep rose before him.

Just a few more feet. Cam whispered a quick prayer as blackness engulfed him.

Chapter 8

"Hurt?" Fiona clutched the arm of the man before her. "Where is he?" *Oh, dear God*. Panic sucked the breath from her as she wildly searched the main hall for Cam.

She gripped Timothy's *liene* and dragged his face down to hers. "*Where is he*?" she growled.

He gently removed her hands from his shirt. "In his chamber, being tended by Brae."

She sighed. "I'm sorry—"

Timothy held up his hands. "Go to him."

Tears welled in her eyes. "Aye."

She raced up the stairs and barged into Cam's chamber.

"Och, Fiona," he said as he quickly jerked the bed covering over his body.

Brae chuckled. "The lad is as naked as the day he was born, lass."

After she released a sigh of relief, Fiona took a moment to run her gaze over his shoulders, to where the blanket covered his hips. *Aye, bare enough*. As her gaze traveled along his torso, she gasped. "Cam, your side."

He grimaced as he shifted. "'Tis a wee scratch."

Blood oozed from the cuts on his body. "Stop moving." She grabbed a rag and dipped it into water. "Help me, Brae. We must clean the cuts before we stitch the stubborn man up."

"Aye, Fiona." Brae winked at Cam. "'Tis what I was doing when you entered as if the devil were chasing you." She tsked, examining his wound. "How many men did you fight off, lad?"

He winced. "Not enough." His gaze shifted to Fiona. "Do you think I could have some whiskey before you take the needle to my side?"

"You heard him, lass. Go fetch a dram," Brae instructed.

His jaw had clenched and tight lines rimmed his eyes. A sword rent him from chest to side. A dirk's blade had slashed at his shoulder, and who kenned where else. Gordon's men had done this to him. They'd threatened her clan, her people. And now Cam lay on his bed bleeding, hurting, although he was brave and strong enough not to let it show too much.

Her heart battered against her chest, seeing him this way. Injured, vulnerable. She covered her mouth so he wouldn't see her cry. Turning toward the door, thankful for a reprieve from the sight of Cam's battered body, she left the chamber on a search for whiskey. If spirits could help him, dull some of the pain she kenned would come with stitching up his many wounds, she'd bring him the entire barrel.

Once she exited the chamber, she leaned against the wall to collect her strength. What was happening? Her heart, mind—och, both—were shattered at the thought of Cam lying in his chamber with such grievous injuries. Tears flowed over her face faster than she could swipe them away.

Still, her mind pushed her emotions aside. The man needed whiskey and 'twas her job to get it for him. Then . . . then she'd let Brae sew him up. And Fiona wouldn't stay. Nay, she'd find something to do—aye, anything to do to keep her mind from him.

She fetched the whiskey. This time she knocked before entering.

"Thank you," Cam said with a grin.

How could he smile when he was wounded and bloodied? She held the dram to his mouth. "Take a sip."

He reached for the dram, tipped it, and drank the contents in one gulp.

"More," he growled.

Her eyes widened.

"Do as he bids, lass. 'Tis many a stitch to be done."

She swallowed and nodded solemnly. "Cam—"

He reached for her hand. The intensity of his gaze had her taking a step forward. "Later, Fiona."

Later. Aye, 'twas right to wait. *Aye.*

Brae gave her a probing glance, then she pulled out the thread and a long needle. Fiona's stomach heaved. Och, she wasn't a weak lass, but she hated needles. More so, she loathed the pain Cam would feel once Brae set the needle to his wounds.

"Whiskey?" Cam asked. Those dark eyes of his didn't leave her and even with his injuries, he didn't bank the desire in his gaze.

How? Even after their discussion on the crag, how could he still want her?

She longed to take the time to thank him for everything he'd done for her. Breakfast, the new *arisaid*, his profession of love. To tell him—tell him her heart wasn't Mal's any longer.

Despite her bravado, she ducked her gaze and silently chastised her body for warming beneath his gaze. He was just a man, she warned. Albeit a strong, devilishly handsome man with dimples, and—

And those eyes of his. 'Twas as if he kens all when he gazes at you. And he'll keep your secrets, but you're not certain because of the way his mouth curls up on one side.

After Fiona brought another dram of whiskey, she paced outside his chamber. Brae refused her request to help. Secretly she was glad, for the stench of blood curdled her stomach.

But as minutes passed by, fear filled her and she nearly reentered the chamber. She had to see if he fared well.

She reached for the door latch, then let her hand fall.

Brae burst through the door and nearly knocked her on her arse.

"Brae, watch yourself."

"What are ye doing standing there like an *eejit*?" The woman shooed her aside so she could pass. "I've things to do."

Fiona squared her shoulders. "I want to see him."

"Lass, go and eat. You'll do the man no good if you faint dead away from hunger."

She rolled her eyes heavenward. "I've a bit of meat on my bones."

"Och, lass. You call that meat?" Brae grabbed her own stomach. "This is meat."

Fiona chuckled. "Let me see him." She tried to push past the auld woman.

Brae shook her head as she wiped her hands on her apron. "Nay. He's worn through and sleeping. If you vex him, you may undo my stitches."

Vex him? She kenned the man was injured and she wouldn't dare do anything to hurt him further. Fiona sighed. "Aye. But bring word at once if he asks for me."

Brae gestured away from the door and Fiona headed toward the main hall.

"One would think you're enamored with the man," she called with a hint of humor in her voice.

Och, of course Brae would try to vex her. 'Twould be ridiculous for her to be enamored with another man. 'Twas too soon to give her heart to another. Truly, what would others think? She wasn't one of those ninny lasses whose hearts pattered for a different man each fortnight. Nay, she was steady, reliable.

So was her heart.

Brae's chuckle reached her as she descended the stairs, but she wasn't going to respond. Instead she entered the main hall and smiled.

Serving lasses were laying out the meal. Others added more mistletoe and holly about the fireplace and any unadorned surface. Children skipped about singing and a few danced where there was enough room. Festive, joyful. Aye, 'twas a typical Christmas at the Sutherland Keep. Mayhap even more so with the new Lady of the keep and wee Mairi.

"Fiona," Lady Rossalyn called. "Come and join us."

Mal and Lady Rossalyn sat at the dais eating their evening meal. Lady Rossalyn looked lovely in her crimson gown, her long dark hair beautifully arranged. And Mal—och, the man was truly the Laird of Sutherland Clan with his dashing good looks and wearing his tartan and blue doublet.

Fiona brushed her hand over her serviceable skirt with a cringe. She must look a wretch.

And how was she to sit beside them with all of the trouble she'd caused? The clan would gawp at them as a wolfhound might watch for meat scraps falling from the table.

"Come, Fiona," Malcolm said in a weary tone.

She took a few steps forward and grabbed a tumbler of ale from a passing serving lass.

"Aye, m'laird."

His gaze snapped to hers and flashed with a bit of concern before they cleared and his broad grin creased his face.

"I've been telling Malcolm of your work with the elders," Rossalyn commented.

He patted Rossalyn's hand and shared a loving glance with her. "Fiona has always had a soft spot for the elders. And we thank her for it."

Fiona sat at the edge of the chair and set the tumbler down. "'Tis my pleasure," she said, though her throat was parched as her nerves stretched. Would he just get it over with?

"Tell her, Malcolm."

He frowned and Fiona's heart clenched. Was he sending her away? Had she caused too much trouble with his new family? Sweat moistened her palms and she rubbed them over her skirt.

Rossalyn elbowed him and he sighed.

Malcolm turned toward her, gathering her hands in his own. "Fiona, I'm an *eejit*."

She gasped. What was he saying?

"Truly, he is," Rossalyn confirmed with a laugh.

The hall became silent. Heat flushed her face as she glanced about. The entire assemblage seemed riveted, an attentive audience following the actors of a play.

Loathe to cause more drama and trying to make amends for her past behavior, she merely shook her head. "Nay, m'laird. 'Tis I who was a fool." She shifted toward him. "We spoke about this in your chamber."

"Nay, Fiona. He's a fool for letting you worry and fash yourself. He should have given a punishment and we'd be past it. But nay. He didn't make a decision and you have fretted since. I can tell."

The laird had decided on a punishment? What if he were to send her away? Where would she go?

A hum began in the main hall as if the clan grew bored by the actions on the dais. The children began singing once again and a piper joined them. A few men moved some tables and more of the clan musicians began playing their instruments.

Malcolm squeezed her hand, his head dipped down. Then he lifted his gaze and his eyes were riddled with regret and sadness. "I've treated you badly." He looked a bit sheepish.

Lady Rossalyn slapped his arm. "Men," she grumbled, though she flashed a smile.

"It took my lady to show me the error of my ways. I am so sorry, truly sorry. You have been my dear friend for as long as I can remember." A quirk of his mouth revealed the flash of the young lad he'd been when they raced horses. "I will not punish you too harshly." He glanced at his wife.

She smiled as if encouraging him. "You will help in the stables for the next fortnight. Then you can continue with the elders."

Her nerves settled and she sighed with relief. "You are being kind, m'laird." A fortnight in the stables wasn't harsh in the least.

With this Rossalyn snorted, then flushed a bright red. "Sorry, m'laird." She winked at Fiona, clearly indicating she wasn't sorry in the least.

The entire time Malcolm held her hands, she waited for it. The tingly feeling, that rush of heat and the desire to never let go. The pang of a heart suffering the excitement of love.

She furrowed her brow; willed her body to respond.

A moment passed. Still she waited.

"Fiona?"

She cleared her throat and returned Mal's gaze, straightened a bit, and released a sigh. Thoughts raced through her mind. Memories of her trailing after Mal and Cam. Those times when she thought she couldn't breathe unless she was near him. And the stab of betrayal when he told her he'd wed Rossalyn. As strange as it seemed, a sense of calm drifted over her. Peace. Comfort. And the urge to let go. Let go of it all. "Not to worry, Mal," she said, surprised by her thoughts and even more so her words.

He brightened and released her hands. "You forgive me?"

Rossalyn leaned forward with an eager expression on her face.

Fiona laughed at his shock. "Aye. But you've done nothing for which I have to forgive."

Meeting Rossalyn's eyes, Fiona couldn't help but think how the gentle woman had changed Mal—for the better, certainly. He'd always been kind to the people of the clan, but a happiness surrounded him, softened him.

He stood and pulled her into an embrace.

"You are a gracious woman." He kissed her brow. "You will find love, Fiona. I ken you will," he whispered in her ear.

Rossalyn came beside them and pushed her way into their embrace. "I am so happy you have settled your differences."

Malcolm roared with laughter. "As if you'd let me do otherwise, wife."

She gave a graceful lift of her shoulders and a knowing smile curled her lips. "And now Fiona can focus on securing herself a husband."

"Lady Rossalyn!" Heat flooded Fiona from neck to hairline. "I do not need a husband."

Again Lady Rossalyn and Laird Malcolm shared a look. One of those smug asides that told her they completely disagreed with what she said. Och, they vexed her.

Malcolm's expression grew serious and his eyes darkened. "How is Cam? When I checked on him, Brae was sewing his side."

"She wouldn't let me see him." Fiona tried to keep the pout out of her tone.

Again the happy couple shared a knowing glance.

"I'll check on him and let you ken how he is fairing. He led the men with strength and sent all of those injured back with no regard to himself."

She'd heard the stories of his bravery. How he'd taken on several men and had been hurt in the process. Kevin had told the story with great flourish and even re-enacted the fight showing Cam as the victor.

Och, why did he risk himself? She shook her head. She kenned the answer. As Sargent-at-Arms, he led the men by example. He'd never expect another clansman to risk all without doing so himself. He was braw, truth be told.

A braw man, indeed.

A serving lass arrived and whispered in Rossalyn's ear as she kept her eyes on Fiona. What the devil?

Worry flashed over Rossalyn's face, then she frowned. "I'll see to him right away."

Mal stood and moved to her side. He set his hand upon her shoulder. "What is the matter, my love?"

In her gut she kenned, without Lady Rossalyn saying a word.

Regardless, Lady Rossalyn murmured, "'Tis Cam."

Fiona stood and her chair tumbled backward. "What?"

"He's fevered."

She clutched her chest and started toward his chamber, striding quickly, then broke out into a run. She threw the door open and froze in place.

Brae mopped his brow with a cloth, tsking as she did so. "I'll sit with him."

The older woman offered a kind smile as she rose. "Aye, lass." Brae slowly straightened and moved away from the bed. Fiona swallowed and accepted the cloth the woman handed her.

"I'll see fresh water and some tea is brought to you."

"Thank you," she said without taking her gaze from Cam.

He began to thrash about the bed, twisting the blankets between his legs. Fiona straightened the blanket, tucking them back under his chin.

"Och, the blasted mule. He'll tear the stitches." Brae hurried to Cam's side. "Come, lass. Talk to him, try to settle him."

With shaking hands Fiona touched his forearm. She jerked her hand away at the heat of his skin. The man was burning hot.

"Lass!"

"Aye." She leaned down close to Cam's ear. "I ken you let me win. I kenned it at the time, but didn't want to give you the satisfaction." With a smile, Fiona remembered their races, be it on horse, foot, or in the loch. "'Twas sweet of you. A true gentleman, Auld David said."

She sat upon the edge of his bed and took the cloth from Brae. She dipped it in the bucket of cool water and wrung it out. "The way you protect the clan," she continued as she wiped his brow, "makes us feel so safe. Truly safe. You are a braw warrior, Cam."

Tears seeped into her voice as he stopped thrashing. "Please, Cam. Please fight this fever. For the clan."

For me.

"Keep talking to him, lass. He needs to hear your sweet voice."

Fiona had never been told she had a sweet voice. Shrewish? Aye. Loud? Aye. Never sweet.

She re-wet the cloth and patted down Cam's brow and face. Tight lines rimmed his eyes, bracketed his mouth. His pale skin was so gray, she feared he was near death. Sweat drenched his chest and soaked the sheets. 'Twould need to be changed, but she worried moving him would cause him pain and start him bleeding once again.

Her stomach clenched and her heart pounded against her chest. "Cam," she said softly. "Do you remember when we ate all of Cook's pies right before Timothy was to wed? Och, she was so filled with ire." She chuckled. "'I'll whip yer arses,' she'd yelled at us. Then we ran so fast she couldn't keep up." The memory was so dear and so reminiscent of their youth together. One day they worked alongside each other in harmony, the other they were causing mischief and pointing the finger of fault at each other.

Mostly, they helped each other grow and survive their losses and troubles, but celebrate joyful events as well.

"I remember your mother made you pay," Brae said.

Aye, that she did. Fiona couldn't sit for three days and she had to fetch whatever Cook wanted for a fortnight. Still, 'twas fun while they were stuffing their faces with apple and berry pies. Although, Cam had lost his stomach most of the night.

"I loved when we escaped to the glen and sat beneath the afternoon sun, jesting with each other." At those moments they shared their secrets and fears, and more importantly their greatest hopes.

Fiona had never voiced it, but her greatest hope was to be lady of the keep. 'Twas what drove her, drove her to follow Malcolm and try to get him to notice her enough to fall in love with her.

And now, here she sat with Cam and Malcolm was with his wife.

Strange how the hopes of one so young changed when life threw an obstacle in the way.

She slipped her hand in his and squeezed. "Cam, what you said in the forest? I didn't mean to hurt you. I never wanted that." How she regretted her harsh response to him. Worse, it wasn't how she felt. He'd frightened her with his vehemence, the bold honesty behind his words.

His hand, bronzed from the sun, engulfed hers. She felt every callus, a bump on the finger he broke during his first sparring event. Fiona placed her other hand over his and prayed.

When she opened her eyes, Brae was gone and 'twas just her and Cam.

For hours she wiped his brow and softly recounted all of their antics from as far back as she could remember. People came and went, brought fresh water and food, words of concern.

Brae begged her to rest, but Fiona pushed her away.

"How is he?"

She turned toward the door and saw Malcolm and Rossalyn standing there. She scraped her hair from her face and shook her head. "Still fevered."

"You need to rest," Mal said as he moved to Cam's bedside, touched his forehead. "*Bollocks*. Burning hot."

Tears shimmered in Rossalyn eyes. "We'll pray for him, Fiona."

Not trusting herself to speak, she kept her gaze on Cam. Rest could wait.

"Aye. We will," Malcolm said. His eyes met hers and fear lingered in their depths. The same fear spiked her heart with dread. Their dear friend was injured, suffering, and there was little they could do. Mal straightened and his jaw flexed. "I'll send more food for you and fresh water for Cam."

"Thank you," she whispered.

Rossalyn grabbed his hand and dragged him from the room. "Let's go to the kirk first."

A small smile played on Fiona's mouth, thankful for the laird and his wife and their offer of prayer. She continued to speak to Cam, wipe his brow.

Beyond exhausted, she slipped into the bed, lay next to him, setting her hand atop his chest just to feel the intake of his breath. Her fears nearly consumed her, but she needed to have strength for both of them, since Cam had used his strength to help the clan in their time of need.

Her last memory was of curling closer and falling asleep.

Cam jerked awake and moved to get up. His muscles groaned.

"Damn," he muttered. His flesh pulled tight against Brae's stitches as he tried to rise once again. Sweat drenched his forehead and ran down his back. He fell back onto the bed and with a panting breath, swore.

He'd kill for water.

But he remained still, then drifted into a fitful sleep.

Flashes of memories came to him. A soft voice, a

feminine touch, and then warm curves pressed against his side.

Who? When? Why?

As his eyelids lifted to blurry slits, Brae bustled in with a few serving lasses.

"Set the water over there, lass. Quiet, we don't want to bother Cam."

"Too late," he muttered.

Brae squealed. "Och, Cam." She rushed to his side and touched his brow. Her wide grin greeted him like the blaring sun on a summer day. "Your fever has broken."

"Water."

"You heard the man, water it is."

He winced at her booming voice.

She shrugged. "Sorry, Cam."

The serving lass brought him a ladle of cold water. He took a gulp.

"Sip it," Brae warned him. After three ladles his thirst was finally quenched.

"'Tis many who've been worried about you, lad." She nodded toward his back. "Let me have a look at the stitches."

Cam rolled onto his side, hissing as he did so.

"Gather my cloths, lass." One by one, Brae cleaned his wounds as he winced each time he had to move.

"Thank you," he said when she was done torturing him. He maneuvered onto his back and tried to catch his breath. His strength was gone.

"'Tisn't me you need to thank, lad." She grinned and winked. "Gather his morning meal."

The lass left the chamber and quickly returned with porridge.

He swatted at Brae's hand when she tried to feed him. "How long?"

The older woman frowned. "For what?" She waved away the serving lass.

He swallowed, his throat still parched. "I feel like I've been here a fortnight."

She laughed. "Nay, just over five days."

"*Five days*." He struggled to rise, despite the pain and fatigue. What a blasted fool he was. He'd never been abed this long, even with worse injuries.

Brae set a hand on his chest and pushed him back down. "Stay in bed."

"You've tended over me enough."

She chuckled and shook her head. "Twasn't me, lad."

He narrowed his gaze as he stood, then reached for the wall to steady himself. After he caught his breath, Cam demanded, "Who?"

"Och, lad," she said with an exasperated look on her face. "Use the mind God gave you."

Was it Fiona, whispering stories of the youth as she bathed his forehead with cool water? Was it her soft touch and even softer curves he'd felt?

"Aye," Brae said when he widened his eyes. "The lass nearly wore herself out tending over you. Wouldn't rest until Malcolm came and yelled the rafters down."

She'd nursed him back to health. The woman whose stomach churned at the sight of blood. And while she tended the elders, sickness wasn't something she favored helping with. "I must go to her."

The auld woman stood before him with her arms crossed over her chest. "You need to rest."

"But—"

She held up her hand. "Cease vexing me, lad. I'll send for her."

Once she left the chamber, Cam sat on the edge of his bed. Fiona had tended him? The dulcet tone of her voice still resonated in his mind. 'Twas as if an angel had shared the most beautiful of stories as his body healed and the pain had begun to lessen. It almost seemed the heat of her touch remained. Or was it merely his imagination wishing it were so?

He grinned at the thought of Fiona sitting at his side, tending him. How he longed for someone to take care of, who would in turn care for him. A wife. A lover. The mother of his future bairns.

Children with her bewitching green eyes and that grin, half vexed and half humored. Lads and lasses who worked hard and were determined. Aye, determined to drive him mad, he imagined.

With a quick shake of his head, Cam rubbed his stubbly chin and looked at the door.

Waiting for her to enter.

Waiting for the woman he loved.

Chapter 9

Mal filled a glass with wine, took a sip and then handed it to Rossalyn. The glance between them made Fiona's heart ache for such a love, a connection.

"Come, Fiona," Mal said. "Drink some wine. Enjoy, for we will be celebrating Christmas soon." He wiggled his brows. "And our Cam is on the mend."

Cheers rang out and she glanced wistfully at the tree festooned with candles and balls of mistletoe.

Aye, Christmas.

Och, she didn't understand what was bothering her. 'Twas as if something was missing.

Or someone.

A wide-eyed serving girl rushed over. "You must come, Fiona," she said with a panicky voice.

She stood, nearly knocking the table from the dais. "Is he . . . is—"

The lass pulled at her arm. "I ken naught. Lillian told me Brae said you must come. Now."

Fiona raced to his chamber, bumping into anyone who stood in her path. The pounding of her heart was deafening in her own ears. *Please God*, she prayed. She stumbled to a stop at the door, gripping her hands together. Painful breaths rushed from her mouth as she tried to gulp in air. She couldn't swallow past the tears clogging her throat. She'd never said the words. Never told him after she'd been so cruel.

"'Tis time you've come," Brae said as she approached from down the hall. Her drawn face was too serious and fear gripped Fiona's heart once again.

Tears filled her eyes. "Is he—is he—?"

"Och, lass." The auld woman patted her arm. "Go and see him."

Shoving the door open, dread had Fiona dragging her feet as she approached his bed. No amount of might could make her eyes look further. She closed them tightly.

"Fiona?"

Her eyes flew open as her gaze snapped to the bed. There lay Cam, propped up against pillows, his chest bare, sporting bruises and bandages.

"Cam!" She launched herself into his arms.

His strong arms wrapped around her, held her tight. She inhaled deeply and smiled.

Aye, home.

Fiona pulled back and looked at the man. A good man. One who helped all without question. A man who'd let the spoiled lass of her youth win, just to see her joy. "Am I hurting you?"

He grinned and his eyes flashed with a devilish gleam. "Nay."

Her heart soared.

"Mayhap a wee bit." He moved over in the small bed and she perched on the end.

"I'm sorry!"

As he smoothed her hair from her face, she whispered, "I thought . . . I thought you'd . . . I thought I'd lost you."

"Nay, my love. I am on the mend because of you. Brae said you stayed with me the entire time."

She ducked her gaze. "Aye."

"Why? Why, Fiona?" He spoke quietly with wonder and a trace of humor in his tone.

"I love you," she blurted.

Cam laughed. "I ken."

She drew back with a pout. Cam bent to her and kissed her temple. "Nay, do not be vexed." He brushed her hair from her brow. "I kenned you loved me when you insisted on nursing me through the night." His smiled wavered. "'Twas dear, you ken. And when I woke, there was something in my mind, memories of a lass sleeping beside me."

Her skin flushed. She looked into his eyes. "You remembered?"

Cam kissed the tip of her nose. "Aye. And Fiona, I never want to spend a night without you at my side."

"Cam," she whispered.

"Be mine, Fiona."

Tears welled. "Aye."

He cupped her face with his strong hands. Hands she knew would keep them steady as they wed, welcomed bairns, and grew old together.

He pulled her close, kissed her. Heat raced through her as she gazed at him. Tiny lines fanned around his smiling eyes. Falling into the love shining from within him, Fiona pulled him closer and slanted her mouth against his.

He growled and rolled her onto her back. Without parting their lips, Cam smoothed his hand over her shoulder, along her side. She shivered at the pleasure his touch wrought. Her heart pounded with anticipation and excitement.

"Cam, your injuries."

Desire darkened his gaze and tensed the line of his jaw. "'Twould hurt more if you stopped."

Cam continued to explore her body with his strong hands. The rough calluses on his fingers pressed through the worn linen of her shirt. Heat pooled deep within her, filling her with such stark desire, it felt as if she'd surely expire from such pleasurable feelings.

"Ah, Fiona," Cam whispered against her mouth. "I have dreamed of this for so long."

He slipped her *liene* over her shoulder, exposing her breast. She blushed beneath his steady gaze.

"You are so beautiful." He moved and winced.

"Cam, you'll hurt yourself." She touched the bandage along his shoulder, then let her hand fall.

His grin was sensual and wicked. "'Twould take an army to stop me."

She laughed, marveling how his smile and steady gaze made her feel as if she were loved. Emotion overwhelmed her, sensations charging through her body. All because of this man. Once again she laid a hand on his shoulder, carefully slipped off the bandage, and peered at the jagged stitching. Reddish and puckered, but healing nonetheless.

"I'm fine, lass."

Her brow quirked. "I'll be the judge of that."

A flash of a sensual grin, then Cam rose over her, kissed along her jaw, down her neck and hovered at the cleft between her breasts.

She arched and moaned as he attended to her body.

"Aye, lass. Do you like my touch?"

His hands trailed to her breasts, cupping the weight of them.

She whispered, "Aye."

"Lovely," he murmured against her skin.

She wiggled as his whiskers tickled the sensitive flesh. He started to slip off her skirt. Panic flared for a moment, then banked when he continued to whisper to her.

"I love you." He cupped her chin. "Always ken how much I love you."

The sincerity of his tone and the way he looked at her—as if he longed to devour her one minute and cradle her in his arms forever—had her helping him push her skirt aside.

"Are you certain?" he asked, his jaw clenched, his hands trembling as he moved them over her body.

She reached up and touched his face. "Aye." She wanted him with a fierceness which surprised her. Never had she felt such need and longing for him to be hers. It surprised her nearly as much as it delighted her that she'd finally made the right decision when it came to the man she loved.

He tossed her skirt off the bed. Cam smoothed his hands down her stomach, over her hips. She gasped as he kissed her mound. He glanced up and winked. Then pain flared in his eyes as he shifted and rose over her.

"We can wait until you are well." Just as she said the words, she wished he'd chide her for thinking of stopping.

"Nay!" he growled as he rid himself of the short britches Brae had put on him.

There he stood with nary a stitch of clothing. His wounds marked him angrily, but she could still admire the fine man he was. Broad of shoulder, muscle bound arms and legs with deep planes of toned muscles. A lean waist and hips. And . . . and his manhood, ramrod straight.

Lines bracketed his mouth and he winced as he returned to the bed. He climbed over her like a wild cat stalking its prey. A sheen of sweat coated his skin.

"You're overworking yourself," she admonished. She dragged her finger along his shoulder and over his arm, admiring the hardness of his muscles and the dips and valleys between them.

Cam chuckled and rested his forehead against hers. "Nay, 'tis my desire for you."

She grinned, then glanced down at him. *Oh, dear.* Without thinking of it, she frowned.

"Not to worry, lass. I'll go easy."

Even though a heated blush rose over her chest and face, those words filled her, made her ache for him, need him with an urgency she didn't ken how to describe. All she knew was that heat seeped from her, liquid heat.

She splayed her palm over his chest, moved it to cover his heart. *Thump, thump*—it beat in tandem with hers. *I'm yours*, it seemed to say. A predatory claim urged her to arch up and kiss him. She wanted him, wanted him to be hers only. She moved her mouth over his, softly, then more insistently. He slid his tongue along her lips, tracing them. A shiver of pleasure raced down her spine. When he parted his lips against hers, a heady sensation overcame her.

She pulled him closer, down upon her body. Och, the weight of him, the hard planes of his muscles against her, heated her like the huge fire after harvest.

Slowly he eased into her. Fiona stiffened. He nuzzled her neck and whispered, "I love you, Fiona." As he moved, she shifted. After a few moments of his gentle administrations, tendrils of pleasure began to roar through her blood. She lifted her hips, wanting him closer, deeper.

The heat of him surrounded her. She sighed as he eased in and out. She held him tight against her, loving how his hard muscles seemed to yield against her skin. As if they were melding into one.

"What are you doing to me?" she moaned as pressure and pleasure built.

"Wait, my love, and you will see." He suckled her peaked nipples, drawing them deep into his hot, moist mouth.

She cried out; gripped his shoulders. Wave after wave rumbled through her. She gasped, trying to hold on, cling to the shattering pleasure exploding within her.

"Let it come, Fiona. Let it come." He sheathed himself to the hilt, arching his neck as he growled his release.

He collapsed beside her, their chests heaving, her body still singing.

"I am yours, Cam."

Epilogue

She took his breath away. Fiona, his bride, his wife-to-be, walked toward him on the eve of Christmas. Her red hair was twined about her head with white flowers tucked within the fiery strands. 'Twas an angel gliding toward him. An angel dressed in a gown of green, the clan plaid draped along her shoulder.

She made Cam prouder than he'd ever been.

Her cheeks stained red as he held her gaze. Her lovely eyes shimmered with tears, he kenned from happiness.

How had it happened, the miracle of her love? All of his hopes and dreams, coming toward him, holding a bouquet wrapped with ribbons. Just as Fiona was to him, a gift wrapped with beautiful ribbons.

He reached for her, his arm outstretched for her to clasp his hand and come forward to be his wife.

Once her fingers were safely cradled within his own, Cam pulled her tight against his side and vowed to never let her go.

"You are lovely," he whispered before the priest started the ceremony.

"As are you," came her witty retort.

Cam threw his head back and laughed. God, his heart was full and he kenned the right woman for him was at his side.

As the priest said the words, all he could think about was *Fiona, Fiona, Fiona.*

"You may kiss your bride."

The clan roared.

Cam lifted Fiona into his arms and strode from the clan kirk, headed toward the keep.

Clansmen laughed and cheered. "That's a lad, Cam. Show her who's master."

A woman swatted at him as they passed. "Let the poor lass eat. She'll need her strength with a lad such as you."

More laughter and ribald jokes.

She ducked her head against his doublet. "Cam, we need to attend the feast," she muttered with a mix of eagerness and mortification.

Her green eyes never left his and in those stunning depths he saw love and desire.

He saw his future.

"Nay, Fiona." He paused so he could kiss her full lips. "All I need is to make you mine by Christmas."

About The Author

Madelyn Hill has always loved the written word. From the time she could read and all through her school years, she'd sneak books into her textbooks during school in order to devoured books daily. At the age of 10 she proclaimed she wanted to be a writer. After being a "closet" writer for several years, she sent her manuscripts to publishers and is now published with Soul Mate Publishing. And she couldn't be happier! A resident of Western New York, she moved from one Rochester to another Rochester to be with the love of her life. They now have 3 children and keep busy cooking, watching sports, and of course reading.

Authors love to hear from readers!

Please connect with Madelyn
Facebook: https://www.facebook.com/madelyn.hill.94
Twitter: https://twitter.com/AuthorMaddyHill
Website: www.madelynhill.com

Other books by Madelyn Hill
Wolf's Castle (2014) - https://www.amazon.com/dp/B00KWO4B4K
For The Love Of A Gypsy (2015) - https://www.amazon.com/dp/B00VG98NWQ
Heather In The Mist (2015) - https://www.amazon.com/dp/B015EFRB6G
Highland Hope Book 1 of the Wild Thistle Trilogy (2016) - https://www.amazon.com/dp/B01I06XNX6